FLIGHT
OF THE
FISHERBIRD

Map of San Juan Islands, 1866

Whatcom Wharf, about 1880

For Judy Stokes and Michele Corriel with love

First published in Great Britain in 2004 by Bloomsbury Publishing Plc
38 Soho Square, London, W1D 3HB

First published in America in 2003 by Bloomsbury USA Children's Books

Text copyright © Nora Martin 2003
The moral right of the author has been asserted

A CIP catalogue record of this book is available from the British Library

ISBN 0 7475 7115 5

Printed in Great Britain by Clays Ltd, St Ives plc

1 3 5 7 9 10 8 6 4 2

All papers used by Bloomsbury Publishing are natural, recyclable products
made from wood grown in well-managed forests. The manufacturing processes
conform to the environmental regulations of the country of origin.

FLIGHT
OF THE
FISHERBIRD

NORA MARTIN

BLOOMSBURY
CHILDREN'S
BOOKS

CHAPTER 1

August 1889

Seven days of rain.
Fourteen days born in fog.
Twelve days clear with a breeze that is new from the ocean.
One day with a death.

It was a tight quiet that pressed down on the people in the church. Rustling clothes and whispered voices hovered like the dust particles that floated in the window light. Clem looked down at her farm-stained hands clasped together over her cotton dress. Never having been to a funeral before, she felt as squeezed and suffocated as the body that lay in the coffin at the front of the room. To keep her mind busy she silently recited her list:

Seven days of rain . . .

Making lists was one of her favorite things to do.

Outside, summer drizzle chilled the grassy fields and the distant pockets of fir trees. Clem gazed out of the church windows toward the San Juan Islands. They looked like resting whales in the waters off the Washington coast. Just thinking about her home on Granger Island made Clem glad. Granger Island Farm was a mile long and a mile and a half wide. Her family's property covered the entire island, every inch of it. Clem almost lifted her hand to trace the rounded outlines of the islands on the church window.

Instead she worked her hand into the pocket of her skirt. There her fingers found the fragile piece of madrone bark rolled into the shape of a scroll. The madrone tree sheds the outer layers of its bark like an animal sheds fur. Ever since Clem could remember, this bark had been her paper when she couldn't get the real thing. She rubbed the smoothness of it between her fingers, seeing in her mind the red-brown color of one side and the pale green of the other. The green side was where she made her lists and kept notes on everything that interested her. Clem knew the list in her pocket by heart, as she knew each of the lists she had penciled since she was six. This list was of all the birds she had seen on the island in the last week.

Kingfishers—3
Bald eagles—12
Yellow warblers—9
Cormorants—9
Unknown small brown birds that eat in the woods—23
The fat, almost tailless forest bird—1
Long-legged shore birds—a flock of several dozen
singing a common melody

Clem chanted the list in a whispered song. And then she added, "This is all I know." She knew only some of the names and habits of the plants and animals in the islands. Without books or schooling, she learned only what her parents knew or what the few other people she came into contact with could tell her. She figured that was why many times her lists flooded beyond simple columns of words or facts. Instead, they often streamed into descriptions, hopes, and sometimes even something like a story.

Her mother leaned over and whispered, "It is truly lovely you look today, as nice as any town girl. My little child, thirteen years and three months old." Her mother took her hand.

Clem couldn't feel pretty, ever. She was too long and brown. She remembered her mother telling her.

"It's earth eyes you have," she had said.

"The color of dirt," Clem had complained.

"Yes." Her mother had clung to Clem as if she were afraid she might float away. "Like the soil of the island you were born to. God made this beautiful place that gives us such a blessed life and a beautiful daughter to share it with."

Clem knew she was the measure of her parents' time on the island because she was born just three days after their arrival from Scotland. Left behind them were the graves of five babies, each of whom had died before they were two years old.

Clem squirmed on the hard wooden pew.

"Halfway through eighteen eighty-nine," Pastor Oggleham intoned, "we bid farewell to our friend, Paul Hersey. A man known and loved in our community and all along the Washington coastline. From Tacoma to the Canadian border he was a respected and esteemed man of business."

Clem looked down the row of people to her uncle Doran, Paul Hersey's business partner, and Sarah Hersey, the dead man's daughter. Tears dropped slowly from Sarah's cheeks.

Sarah's sadness was like a fever that spread to everyone in the room. Clem felt her own face tense with sorrow. She had liked Paul. He didn't come often to their farm on Granger Island, or sail with Uncle Doran, preferring to manage the business from his office in Port Townsend. But when he did, he always showed Clem a gentle kindness.

From the back of the church the wooden doors squeaked open, interrupting Pastor Oggleham's eulogy. Every head in the crowded room turned to see who was coming in. Standing in the doorway were four men. Two of them were dressed in the loose-fitting brown pants and matching shirts that were the customary dress of the Chinese. They had long, braided queues at the backs of their heads. The other two were also Chinese but were dressed in American-style work clothes.

Clem had seen Chinese men before; one even worked for her uncle. Also, several Chinese had worked at the lime quarry on nearby San Juan Island until late last year. But for the last several years the government had not allowed any more Chinese workers to come to the United States. Even before the laws, many of the white workers had decided they could get rid of Chinese who were already here. Uncle Doran called the white gangs "Tacoma mobs," after the town where the violence started.

"They enforce their own idea of the law by beating and murdering Chinese," he had said, disgusted. "All along the coast Chinese are being kicked out of their jobs on the railroads and in mines by gangs."

Now Pastor Oggleham asked, his voice skimming over the heads of the congregation like the call of a cormorant over water, "What do you want here?"

One of the men dressed in work clothes stepped forward. "We would pay our respects to Boss Hersey."

A low, whispered growl rumbled through the congregation. Pastor Oggleham looked around nervously. "We don't want trouble, today of all days," he told the Chinese men.

The growl of hatred from the congregation grew louder. Mr. Johnson from Orcas Island stood up and pointed at the Chinese. "Take your yellow hides out of here. Let us mourn our own kind in peace." Around him the murmuring crowd seemed to agree. Even Clem's father nodded.

At first the Chinese men looked angry, then embarrassed, but they remained anchored in the doorway. The man who spoke for them said very quietly, "Paul Hersey was a friend to every man."

Clem heard his words given out like a prayer, but she was sure not many of the others in the church did over the surging voices of complaint.

Mr. Johnson stayed firm, rooted in the congregation's support. "Get out, you squinty-eyed animals!" he yelled.

Pushed out on the wave of angry words, the four men retreated through the doors. The congregation shared whispers of victory before looking again to Pastor Oggleham.

At the end of the service Paul Hersey's body was carried out of the church. A wake of people followed the wagon that hauled the coffin to the cemetery. Slowly, head-bent men and women walked down the pine-scented dirt road, sheltered under wool scarves and large hats. It struck Clem as strange how these strong, energetic people who had caused the ugly ruckus a few moments ago now paraded their mourning postures, like putting on a mask.

Sarah Hersey stayed near her dead father, her face almost as pale as the corpse's. Uncle Doran walked beside the sobbing girl.

Sarah was fifteen, two years older than Clem, but she was shorter and smaller. She seemed to Clem to be like a porcelain doll with round pink cheeks. In comparison, Clem had long arms and legs. Her sleeves and dress hems were always too short. And her thick hair wouldn't stay tucked into a braid. Standing near Sarah, she felt like the long, slim mast on her boat, the *Fisherbird*, back home. Sarah's blue eyes glistened with tears.

At a distance Clem saw a large group of Chinese people standing silently. The four men were amongst them. Slightly in front of the group stood Uncle Doran's deck hand, Ray Chung. Clem had never seen him on shore before. Even when her uncle's boat, the *Doran Bull*, stayed at Granger Island for days at a time, she had never seen Ray Chung leave it. In her mind he had become a part of the ship, like the sails or the ropes. Clem was always a little afraid of Ray Chung. When she sailed on the *Doran Bull*, he moved past her as if she were not there. And Ray Chung never spoke to Clem except to tell her to get out of his way.

Most of the mourners passed without noticing the Chinese, but Mr. Johnson spat in their direction as he went by. The Chinese men looked at their feet as if they didn't see him. All except Ray Chung; he glared back with clenched fists and took a step forward. But, seeing a nod from Uncle Doran, Ray Chung stopped.

Clem let the congregation pass her by. She heard the hushed voices of acquaintances from many of the islands. There were people from San Juan, Shaw, Lopez, and Orcas, and from the smaller islands as well. Everyone knew Uncle Doran and Paul Hersey. Their boat was a floating store. They bought supplies in the mainland towns of Tacoma and Port Townsend, items that were hard for islanders to get, such as dress goods and cooking utensils. Then they sailed the islands selling their wares to farmers and loggers and fishermen. Now Paul was dead.

For a moment Uncle Doran left Sarah and put his arm around Clem. Instantly she felt welcomed and safe. "My favorite niece, tall and good-looking. I'm proud to call you a Nesbitt."

"Uncle Doran." Clem knew the joke. "I'm your only niece."

He laughed in his smooth, easy way and hugged her. "I just wanted to give you this." He handed Clem several paper labels from canned goods. Paper was scarce and expensive. What little Clem's family had was used to write letters to family members still in Scotland, or business correspondence. So Uncle Doran often saved slips of paper for Clem to use for her jottings, as he called them.

"Thank you." Clem put them in her pocket, planning

to make a list of all the islands she could see as soon as the funeral was over.

Uncle Doran said, "Enjoy, niece. I must comfort poor Sarah now. She has lost both her mother and father in her short lifetime." Uncle Doran stepped away to resume his place beside Sarah.

Although Clem had met Sarah several times before, visiting in Port Townsend, she couldn't find the courage to speak to her now. What were the right words to say on this sad day? They had never been friends. Mentally, Clem listed the things Sarah had that she didn't:

> *Schooling with books*
> *Golden hair that moves gently*
> *Blue eyes*
> *Teachers to answer every question*
> *Science class*
> *Friends*
> *School!*

Interrupting Clem's thoughts, her mother said, "Your Uncle Doran is asking if we will take Sarah home with us until the spring. Then he'll be taking her to her grandmother in San Francisco."

"Sarah? Live with us?" A nervous tingle spread up Clem's arms, neck, and cheeks. Her shoulders drooped in disappointment as she stared at her mother.

"I think it will be just the thing Sarah needs right now," her mother went on, not noticing Clem's concern. "She is without any family."

"It will be good for you, daughter," her father added as he came to stand beside Clem. "Like having an older sister about."

There was uncertainty in her father's words. Clem knew he was concerned about her. Just a few weeks ago she had overheard him talking to her mother when they thought she was asleep.

"It's my fault, Fanny, that she acts more like a boy," her father had said. "I let her run free over the island all these years, fishing and sailing as if she were a son. If it weren't for you making her learn to read, write, and do her needlework, I'm afraid she'd be completely wild."

Clem could hear her mother's need in the sound of her voice. "She is all we have, Joseph. It is natural that she would be both daughter and son to you. And that we would be holding her dear."

"Other girls her age are already planning their futures, preparing to be good wives and mothers. Our lass is so shy that when she gets off the island she can barely speak to the few people she meets. It's nothing she knows of the world beyond this farm. Perhaps, Fanny," her father continued hesitantly, "we should be sending her to school as she wants."

"We have talked about this before," her mother had answered. "I won't be sending Clementine to the mainland to school. I can't have my only surviving child leave me. She will learn what we can teach her here."

"I know," her father had said. Clem could see in her mind her father putting his understanding hand on her mother's shoulder. "But what we can teach her may not be enough."

Clem had silently begged her mother, *Listen to Papa, please. I'll come back. I would never leave you for good. But if only I could go to school and learn for a few years. There's so much to know!* All the things she wondered about blew through her mind like stormy wind picking up waves. She dreamed of spending her whole life seeing and knowing about everything that was under her feet and within her view.

I could truly be like the sons you lost, Clem had silently pleaded with her parents. *Give me a chance and I could take care of you when you are old.* They had been through all of this before. Her mother could not part with Clem, and her father did not believe in women doing a man's work on the farm.

Now her mother and father were waiting for her response about Sarah. Before Clem thought much about her words she mumbled, "I don't want her to be a sister."

"Clementine! How can you be so cruel?" Her mother's face looked shocked. "Sarah is an orphan now. It is the least we can do for her and for Doran. She certainly can't stay at his bachelor's cabin."

It was settled. Sarah would live with them through fall and winter, and into next spring. Clem had no choice.

CHAPTER 2

Islands Seen from the Deck of the
Doran Bull

Spiden, San Juan, Lopez, Reid, Shaw
The high top of Orcas
The tiny dots that have no names
Spirit Island in a shawl of morning mist
Our home, Granger, reaching out with joy across the gray waves

Clem planned out in her mind the list she would make until her attention was brought back to the funeral by her mother's voice. "Clementine, please, tell Sarah you are glad she will be coming with us."

As Clem walked toward where her uncle and Sarah were standing, a man suddenly cut in front of her. Her uncle's greeting showed Clem that they knew one another.

"Clark," her uncle said, nodding. "A strange place for a Revenuer."

"Revenuer" was another name for the Border Patrol

Police who guarded the waters between the United States and Canada, looking for whiskey smugglers. Smugglers were dangerous. Clem's father called them pirates. He had told her, "Men like that will slit your throat if you happen to get in their way." It always made Clem shiver to think about it.

"Paul Hersey's death was a tragic accident," Officer Clark told Clem's uncle. "How do you suppose it happened?"

"We think he slipped on the deck and went over," Uncle Doran returned calmly. "He was on watch that night. Ray Chung and I were below. We heard the splash, but when we pulled him in he was dead."

"Dr. Bailey said half his head was crushed," Officer Clark said, eyeing her uncle.

"He must have knocked his head on the side as he fell," Uncle Doran answered. His voice became wary. He put his large, comforting hand on Sarah Hersey's back.

"Or was hit by something before going over," Officer Clark suggested. "Are you sure your Chinaman was below with you that night?" He nodded back in the direction of Ray Chung.

Clem felt her heart speed up with sudden shock. Officer Clark sounded as if he didn't believe Paul fell overboard. What was he saying? Did he think Ray Chung killed Paul?

Clem glanced at Sarah to see her reaction to the policeman's insinuations. But she didn't seem to hear any of the conversation. Her eyes just stared blankly at the wooden coffin in the wagon bed.

Officer Clark continued talking about Ray Chung. "We've managed to get rid of a lot of those yellow men with the Exclusion Act, but we know that they are being smuggled in. Kinda figures one Chinaman might be helping others."

Clem saw that Uncle Doran's expression didn't change as he listened to the man. But when Uncle Doran answered, his voice was hard and forced like gravel grinding underfoot. "Ray Chung has sailored with me for ten years." That was all he said. Uncle Doran walked away from Officer Clark, leading Sarah as he went. The air around him was stiff with his anger. Clem could feel it, and she wondered that the policeman didn't jump back.

It was then that her mother beckoned to her. Clem saw her parents talking to a man with a boy.

"Is this your daughter, Joseph?" the man asked Clem's father.

"This is our Clem," said her father, introducing her. "Clemmy, this is Mr. Parsons and his boy Jed from over on Lopez."

Mr. Parsons added to the introduction. "We came in a neighbor's boat, so I left the missus and the other boys back on the farm."

As Clem searched for an idea to start a conversation with the boy, Jed Parsons jumped right in. "I seen ya out crabbing last week." Jed sounded as easy as if they were already good friends. He was shorter than Clem and his brown hair was shaggy.

Clem longed for friends but didn't know how to get acquainted. It was one of those things her mother said took practice.

The boy's face blushed a little bit, but he continued to talk. "It's a jump-fast fine dory you have. I seen it when I was going over to San Juan with my pa and my brothers. I got three brothers, all littler than me. We bought sheep over on San Juan last spring. Did you make your own crab traps?"

Clem tried to wade out from the pull of so many words coming at her so fast. "No," Clem heard herself say. "My uncle Doran made the crab pots for me."

Her mother smiled encouragement at her. That made Clem feel braver.

"My pa says you got the most shiny-nice farm in the islands," Jed said.

"Granger is the best place in the world." Clem almost smiled at the boy's funny way of talking. It pleased her that her farm was known all through the islands.

"We just have eighty acres right now," Jed said. "Came from Kansas two years ago."

Then her mind went blank. Clem tried to think of more they could talk about: farming, gardening, fishing. Surely there was something they could talk about.

Before she could settle on a subject, Jed stammered, "Well, I—I guess my pa's ready to leave." And he walked away.

"He seems like a nice boy," her mother said, taking Clem's arm.

Later, Uncle Doran escorted Sarah Hersey to the beach. "Clem, here is Sarah. Take her home so you can be sisters."

There's that word again, sister. *It sounds like a plot between my uncle and my father,* Clem thought. She tried to imagine this polished girl in her house, sharing her attic room, wearing farm boots under a ribbon-trimmed dress.

Sarah looked Clem up and down. Clem could feel her eyes measuring every inch. It didn't look as if Sarah liked what she saw either.

"Dear Sarah," Clem's mother said, helping Sarah pull her hooded wrap over her head and around her shoulders. "You must be wrung out. We'll get you home as soon as possible."

"Yes, we should go now to catch the tide," Clem's father said.

Everyone but Clem climbed into Uncle Doran's fifteen-foot dinghy to row out to the big boat. Her uncle's sailing vessel had a large underwater keel to balance it. It had to stay in deeper water, so they used the rowboat to go in and out from shore.

It would be a long day's trip sailing on the *Doran Bull* back to their island, as it had been coming.

Without giving it a thought, Clem waded in the water to shove the dinghy off the beach before jumping aboard herself.

"Your boots and dress, they're soaked!" Sarah said to Clem.

Clem looked at Sarah sitting straight in the center of the boat, her clothes dry and fresh. After Sarah's comment, Clem wished she had let her father push the boat off the beach, but it was habit from when Clem was seven years old and first got her own boat.

When they finally arrived home, Clem's father didn't even light a fire in the stove. They all just went to bed.

It was the very next afternoon after their return when Clem's father told her, "Help your mother in the house as much as you can, Clemmy. Let Sarah be an example to follow while she is with us. Sarah has already shown what a fine cook she is this morning at breakfast."

"Sarah will be a great help to me," her mother confirmed.

An afternoon of housework hung over Clem like a winter drizzle. Somehow sweeping and cooking left her feeling empty. As soon as she was finished the house needed sweeping or a meal needed cooking all over again. She wanted to be outside helping her father or, better yet, exploring the island, looking for new plants or birds she had never seen before. When she found something new she would carefully sketch it onto madrone bark or paper if she had it. Then it would be set in her mind, and if she ever got to go to school there would be books where she would find out the names.

Madrone
Dogwood
Douglas fir

Out of habit Clem started listing in her head the names of trees she already knew. The unfamiliar sight of Sarah starting to clear dishes from the table brought her back to what her father was saying. "With Sarah here," Clem told her father, "I could be helping you."

"I would not want you to waste this chance to be learning from Sarah," he answered. "She is very competent."

"Thank you, Mr. Nesbitt," Sarah said. "I enjoy helping. It keeps my mind off Papa." But as she spoke, Clem saw her lift her chin and look at Clem with a whiff of superiority.

Over the next few days Clem was forced to watch Sarah make a perfect spice cake, whipstitch the buttonholes on the shirt Clem's mother was making, and complete a whole yard of crocheted lace.

"Your needlework is lovely," Clem's mother exclaimed. And then, as if remembering her own daughter, she added, "Clem, you have done very well these past days, a regular young housewife. I think you should be taking the afternoon to enjoy yourself outside."

As Clem put on her boots she watched Sarah smile as if she had some secret and then steal a glance over at her.

Four days she'd been on Granger, and already Clem couldn't stand Sarah. More than anything she wanted to escape the girl.

"Do you need me to come back and help get supper?" Clem asked.

Sarah piped right up. "I'll help you, Mrs. Nesbitt. My father always said I was the best cook he knew." Sarah looked at Clem as if saying again, *I am better than you are.*

"Isn't that nice of Sarah," her mother said to Clem. "That way you can stay out in the *Fisherbird* longer."

The air inside the house felt thick, but Clem hesitated at the door. "Are you sure you don't need me?" she asked again.

Her mother looked at her, puzzled. "This is not like you, Clem. Go on now, take your boat out."

The *Fisherbird* was Clem's seventeen-foot dory. Her father and uncle had built it out of long slabs of wood, curved and nailed one above the other over a frame of sturdy ribs. Then they had varnished it until the wood glistened and painted the trim the dark green of the fir trees.

When it was finished, Clem and her father had named it after the small kingfisher that lived in their islands. Like the bird, the double-ended boat could swoop and dive among the waves without ever losing its balance. When the sails were up and with a stiff wind behind her, the boat felt as if it flew above the sea's surface.

The *Fisherbird* was pulled up onto the beach next to the ten-foot dinghy that her father kept in case of emergency.

"I want that dinghy to be able to come after you, if there be need," he had told Clem. But Clem proved a capable sailor from the moment she first learned to cast off.

"She moves that boat as if it were growing off her backside," Uncle Doran often joked to Clem's father.

As soon as Clem was floating in the bay she felt comforted. The gentle rocking motion of the boat in calm water helped her sort out her thoughts and feelings. She looked back to the house and garden and barn. Clem's love of her home and land wrapped around her like her mother's quilt. She smoothed one of the pieces of paper Uncle Doran had given her and started to write.

Small breeze from the southwest—5 to 8 knots
Low tide, 9 feet of wet beach
Loose, puffy clouds whose bottoms are gray and tops are white

Within minutes Sarah Hersey was forgotten.

CHAPTER 3

What I Want to Know

All the birds and all the plants
What makes one seed grow into a tree and another into a flower
How crabs breathe
Why water changes color
The wind's language

"Good morning," Uncle Doran called as he knocked and opened the front door.

Breakfast dishes clattered as Clem was surprised out of thoughts of a list she was composing. "We didn't expect you until next week at the earliest," she said.

Usually they didn't see Uncle Doran more than once a month, but it had been only five days since Paul's funeral.

"I'm just here for the day," he said. "I was over in Port Townsend yesterday picking up a cargo."

At that moment Clem's mother came down the stairs with Sarah following. "Doran! What a pleasant surprise."

"I stopped by to see how Sarah was feeling." Uncle Doran nodded toward Clem's mother and Sarah.

"I am doing fine, Mr. Nesbitt," Sarah said politely. "Thank you."

"Please, call me Doran," Uncle Doran said. "You are a young lady now." He then took out several packages from his canvas sea bag. "I bring gifts for the ladies."

Forgetting Sarah, Clem moved in excitedly. Uncle Doran always knew exactly what she needed. "First for Fanny," Uncle Doran said as he held Clem back.

"Silk threads," Clem's mother exclaimed. "Now I can continue my embroidery."

"And for my niece." He handed Clem a new lead pencil and a folding pocketknife.

"Thank you, Uncle Doran," Clem said. "My pencil is nothing but a stub." Clem's eyes grew distant as she imagined all the lists she could write with a new pencil and the times she could pull out the new sharp knife to cut fish line or kelp that got tangled in her crab pots. "They're perfect."

Then Uncle Doran announced dramatically, "One last gift." He handed a large package to Sarah. Without giving a thought to what could be inside, Clem stared at the heavy brown paper that covered the gift. Such a big piece of paper! Clem could make a dozen lists with it, maybe even a book's worth of lists. Clem thought of the pictures of plants she could sketch, and without thinking she said aloud, "I could use that."

Sarah scowled at Clem. "You don't even know what's inside." Embarrassed, Clem realized that Sarah thought she coveted her gift instead of the paper it was wrapped in. Clem stepped back as Sarah tore the paper from the gift. A loud *ahh* rang out from both Sarah and Clem's mother. Sarah held up a silk shawl woven from almost invisible shining threads in a rose pattern. "It's the most beautiful thing I've ever seen," she whispered.

It was the most beautiful thing Clem had ever seen as well. She realized she was gripping the pocketknife so hard her fingernails hurt the palm of her hand.

"Oh, Doran, it's exquisite," Clem's mother said softly, touching the fabric.

"Next trip, I will bring you a piece of silk to make a dress to go with it, the color of pink roses. For after your mourning period, of course." Standing behind Sarah, Uncle Doran took the shawl and placed it around her shoulders.

"You know how to charm us ladies," Clem's mother teased.

Clem suddenly hated the pocketknife. In confusion she reached toward Sarah, wanting to feel the soft fabric that encircled the girl.

Sarah saw Clem's hand and stepped backward until she stood wedged tight against Uncle Doran. Clem let her arm drop.

"Now you ladies must excuse me. I need to find Joseph," Uncle Doran said.

"You'll play a game of chess with me before you go?" Clem asked hopefully, knowing her uncle could rarely resist a challenge of any kind.

Several months earlier Uncle Doran had begun teaching Clem the game. But Clem could practice only when Uncle Doran visited. Her father refused to play with her, saying it was a man's game.

Uncle Doran laughed. "You want to lose again?"

"I am getting better," Clem said. "I keep a list of all the new moves I learn."

Uncle Doran hesitated for a moment and then said, "Set up the board, Clem. List or no list, a game with you won't take long."

His eyes teased Clem as he said it, and she rose to the challenge. "One day, Uncle Doran, I'm going to take you by surprise and outmaneuver you."

Clem brought out the homemade chessboard that her uncle and father had played on for years.

"This is a war, Clem." Her uncle set out his pieces. "Sixteen pieces playing on sixty-four squares. Your queen rules over the board, like all strong women." Uncle Doran winked at Sarah as he said this.

Sarah came to stand near Uncle Doran, looking over his shoulder. "I remember my father playing chess with you," she told him. "He said you were one of the best players he'd ever seen." Uncle Doran smiled broadly at the compliment, but Clem could tell his mind was already focused on the beginning of the game.

Clem and Uncle Doran began taking turns moving their chessmen. Rooks, pawns, bishops. Clem moved each piece slowly while her uncle moved with rapid confidence, more often than not taking one of her chessmen captive. Finally Clem fingered her queen. The queen could move anywhere to capture enemy pieces, but it was also the most valuable piece on the board. She didn't want to lose it.

She tried to remember her list of moves, but all she

could remember was never to look at Uncle Doran's face, because she wouldn't believe he was out to take everything.

Think! she scolded herself. What move would Uncle Doran make now? She didn't know. Her fingers moved back and forth from her other pieces to her queen. One last glance at Uncle Doran and she moved her queen forward.

"Clem, Clem, Clem!" Uncle Doran laughed. "You are so predictable. You lose a few men and panic, leaving your queen wide open every time." He captured her queen and two moves later cornered her king. "Checkmate!"

Clem started to pick up the pieces.

"Wait," Uncle Doran stopped her. "Sarah, would you like to learn the game?"

Sarah looked surprised. "Me? It's so masculine." Sarah looked at Clem. "Not suited to a lady at all."

Clem felt the insult that had been aimed at her. She expected Uncle Doran to defend her, but to her surprise he smiled and patted Sarah's hand. "Too aggressive for Sarah. And probably that is good for me. I wouldn't be surprised if our Sarah liked the game once she tried it."

Anger came to a boil in Clem like a pot that had been simmering for a long time—five days, actually. The exact amount of time Sarah had been staying with them. Was Uncle Doran saying Sarah would beat him at chess when it was clear that he thought Clem never would?

"The game does require a great deal of complex thought," Clem said. "Much more than a needle that just goes in and out, in and out."

Right away Clem saw her insult hit Sarah like a well-aimed mud ball. Sarah returned her stare without blinking.

After Uncle Doran left to find her father, Clem went upstairs to the attic room. She fetched her rubber throw-over that she wore when she went fishing and on rainy days. The throw-over was really just a square piece of brown rubber material with a hole cut in the middle for Clem's head.

Sarah came up behind her, rewrapping her new shawl in the paper that Clem wanted. "I am putting this away until I go to San Francisco to live. It's too fine for here." She indicated her embossed leather trunk that sat in the corner under the sloping eaves of the roofline. Clem knew that it was full of Sarah's mother's linens and lace doilies. Sarah had showed Clem every piece that she had carefully folded and laid between layers of thin white paper, with tiny pieces of cedar bark to protect the delicate cloth from moths.

Clem hurried to assemble her fishing gear. She wanted to escape the achy feeling that sloshed around inside her belly when she looked at Sarah and her gift.

On her side of the room sat a wooden box built by her father. Inside it she kept her clothes along with all of her lists, both on scraps of paper and on madrone bark. Almost every list she had ever made since her mother first taught her to write was stored inside the box. Before Sarah had come Clem loved to spend rainy afternoons reading over each one, from the very first, on which she had written in an unsteady childish hand—

My Family
Mumum–1
Daa–1
Uncle Doran–1

Goats—14
Missy Moo Cow—1
Chickens—too many that peck

—to all the lists she had made when she was first learning to sail her boat, the *Fisherbird*:

Port—left
Starboard—right
Bow—front
Stern—back
Let the wind whisper instructions

—to later ones that reminded Clem of complex winds and currents.

Leaving her lists untouched, Clem pulled on the rubber throw-over.

"That smells like the beach at low tide," Sarah said, scrunching up her face.

Already Clem knew that Sarah saved her sweet voice for talking to Clem's parents and now to Uncle Doran. When she spoke to her, Clem always felt as if she were some horrible creature that Sarah couldn't stand to be near. Rats and snakes came to mind.

"It's better than being wet all day from rain or sea spray," she answered.

But Sarah didn't seem to be listening to Clem anymore. Instead she wrapped her arms around her shoulders in a self-hug. "Doran told me I was as beautiful as the finest ladies in San Francisco." Sarah's voice floated around Clem.

"I've never heard Uncle Doran say such things," Clem said.

Sarah stared back at Clem for what felt like a long time. Finally, dropping her voice as if speaking to herself, she responded, "No, I guess you wouldn't."

Clem felt the sharp stab of anger again. Sarah's words brought back Uncle Doran's response to Sarah about learning to play chess. He did treat Sarah differently than he treated her. Clem gritted her teeth. She wasn't going to let Sarah see her upset.

"Doran's a grown man, Sarah, not a boy. He's more than fifteen years older than you."

Sarah half smiled and walked over to the window, where she gazed out to the gray-blue water that held the island in its deep palm. "So?" she said.

"He's just trying to be nice because he feels sorry for you." Clem spat the words out in anger, but they sounded mean.

"We'll see in time," Sarah said. "Won't we?"

Enough, Clem thought. She wouldn't listen to Sarah Hersey talk about her uncle in that way. She wouldn't even lower herself to ask Sarah if she could have the wrapping paper. Clem went pounding down the wood steps, leaving Sarah to fondle her new shawl.

By going to Boulder Beach on the east side of the island, Clem knew she would pass her father and Uncle Doran. Then she'd ask Uncle Doran to go fishing with her. It would be like it used to be between them, before Sarah Hersey and rose-colored silk.

The air was still damp with fog and drizzle blowing in

from the north, but it felt welcome on Clem's face. *It'll make the fish bite better*, Clem told herself. She wound around through the large Douglas fir trees that separated the house from the fields in the center of the island. She checked the blackberry vines for late berries, but all were finished for the season.

Where the trail opened onto the east field Clem stopped and searched for her father and uncle. They weren't hard to find, two giant men rising above the yellow-green stalks of field grass. The grass moved in ripples as if it were wind-lifted waves and the two men were ships afloat on the surface. *Everything is a sea*, Clem thought. *I will make a list of all that reminds me of water.*

The brothers saw Clem coming toward them and waved to her. How much they looked alike, though her father had the lines on his face of an additional ten years of living.

When she was close enough she heard her father say, "Wasn't that man we saw at Paul's funeral with the Border Patrol police? Clark was the name you called him."

"He is," Uncle Doran answered.

"Have you been seeing much trouble in the area?" Clem's father questioned. "The Border Patrol has been passing close to the island every day this week."

"It's not a concern, Joseph," Uncle Doran answered. They stopped talking as Clem approached.

"Uncle Doran, want to go cod jigging?"

"A big chunk of fried cod would taste just about perfect tonight, Clem. I'm tired of Ray Chung's mysterious little bits of this and that he eats with those skinny sticks. But I'm afraid I need to head out before this weather smothers us."

Clem was disappointed, but she knew that following the orders given by water and wind was necessary for them all, especially her uncle, whose business depended on getting from one place to another.

"Next time, Clem," Uncle Doran promised. "In the meantime, you take Sarah out. Show her what a fish line is for."

"I don't think the smell agrees with her," Clem said. She didn't want Sarah brought into the conversation.

Uncle Doran laughed. "The lady does prefer the finer things. She always has, ever since she was a wee thing."

She hadn't thought of it before, but Uncle Doran would know. He had frequently stayed with Sarah and her father in Port Townsend. She was almost like a niece to him. *So why would I feel angry about Uncle Doran bringing her gifts too?* Clem asked herself.

"Well, Clem, even if she won't go fishing, be kind to Sarah for me. She has lost everything."

Uncle Doran's voice soaked her in its goodness. Clem felt terrible about her resentment of Sarah's presence. "I will, Uncle Doran," she promised. As soon as Clem said the words she felt better, like waking up to the channel water smooth as a silver mirror after days of squall.

"I know," Uncle Doran said. "Take her out riding in the *Fisherbird*. Even the fine, finicky Sarah would like that."

Again Clem promised that she would. And after Uncle Doran said good-bye to her father, she watched him walk toward Nesbitt Bay in front of their house, where the *Bull* now lay at anchor.

Boulder Beach wasn't really a beach at all, but a big

jagged rock that jutted out into the deep water of the channel. By perching on the end, Clem could drop a weighted line down where large codfish liked to feed. Then she began jerking it up and down in short hopping motions. That's how this way of fishing came to be called "jigging," like dancing an Irish jig.

By lunchtime, as the wet fog closed in on her, Clem had a large red-scaled cod to take home. Cold and damp, Clem hurried. She frequently had to switch the heavy fish from hand to hand, hooking her fingers inside its gills. Its slimy body slung against her, and she was thankful for her rubber throw-over. She thought suddenly, *Sarah must be right about the smell.* And she laughed.

Entering the woods near her house, Clem promised herself out loud, "I will be nicer to Sarah. I will be like Uncle Doran, good to everyone." It was just as she finished saying this and came around the last tree that she saw them. Uncle Doran and Sarah, sitting close, side by side on a log that marked the beginning of the beach. The fog swirled around them, making Clem think for minute she was dreaming. But then she saw the *Doran Bull* was still in Nesbitt Bay.

Clem stopped, letting the fish slap sharply against her throw-over. The sound caused Sarah and Uncle Doran to look back in her direction.

"I—I thought you had left," Clem stammered to her uncle.

Sarah's cheeks brightened with color, but Uncle Doran smiled. "I found I couldn't let go the opportunity of taking lovely Sarah for a stroll."

"That was a long time ago," Clem mumbled under her

breath. But she was thinking, *He didn't have time to go fishing with me!*

"I do see Ray Chung signaling to me, though." Uncle Doran stood up. He took Sarah's hand as if to shake it. Clem noticed he didn't move it up and down, but just sort of held it for a moment. "Remember, niece," he said, speaking to Clem but looking at Sarah, "you have promised to take Sarah outside while I am gone. I want to see the happiness returned to her face when I get back."

Clem couldn't answer, but silently stood in the shadows behind Sarah as her uncle strode down the beach to his dinghy.

Finally Sarah seemed to notice Clem, covered in fish slime and scales. "What's that?"

"A codfish."

"It's so ugly!" Sarah declared. "I hate cod. Why would you purposely want to catch one?"

"Dinner!" Clem said, lifting the large cod and flinging it into Sarah's surprised embrace. Then she ran away as fast as she could.

CHAPTER 4

Foods from the Sea

Cod and salmon
Clams and oysters
Crabs to feed our bodies
Wind and light
Salty spray and
Water shadows to feed our spirits

Clem didn't return to the house. She hurried straight to the beach and the *Fisherbird*, all her promises of being kind to Sarah forgotten. She pushed hard on the bow of the *Fisherbird*, launching it through a wall of dense fog. Once on the water, Clem put all of her anger against Sarah into rowing away from the shore. She tucked her cotton skirt under her legs and braced her leather boots for added leverage. She could see nothing around her but smooth silver sea mirrored in swirling gray fog. She knew where she was going, where each crab trap waited. But as the boat glided into deeper water, her mind remained tied to Sarah.

Just last night, as she and Sarah had taken turns reading aloud, Clem's father had looked up from the harness he was working on and said to Sarah, "You read that psalm well, miss." Then, turning to Clem, he said, "You would be wise, daughter, to take note of what Sarah can teach you."

Clem saw Sarah glance slyly at her as she responded, "Thank you, Mr. Nesbitt. I hope to be an example to Clementine while I am here. This may be her only opportunity to observe someone who has had the advantages of town society."

But I would go to school if I could, Clem thought desperately.

Clem's father and mother had smiled at Sarah's rude remark. Clem had to stop herself from telling Sarah she saw through her.

Her gentle mother said only, "We are very glad you are here, Sarah. You have also been a great help to me."

"But of course my life in San Francisco will be much different. There I'll have servants," Sarah replied.

"Your grandmother is well off?" Clem's mother asked as she knitted.

"Yes. But even if I live somewhere else," she added, "I'll have servants."

"You have more family in California?" Clem's father asked without taking his eyes off his work.

"In a manner of speaking," Sarah replied.

Clem's thoughts returned to the present as she neared her first crab trap. She found the large floating cork marking her trap. The cork was tied to a line that quickly disappeared into the water. She pulled the wet line hand over hand until a cage made of thin wood slats rose to the surface.

Inside, two large pink crabs and three small ones clambered over one another. Opening the little door, Clem carefully grabbed the bigger crabs from behind to keep from getting pinched. She dropped these into the bottom of the *Fisherbird*, where their sharp pointed legs scraped against the wood and made Clem shiver. She then turned the trap over and shook the small ones back into the water.

"I won't let Sarah spoil my day," Clem promised herself out loud.

Sounds shimmered near Clem, amplified and close as if the tiny particles of noise were trembling in the fog. She let her boat drift toward the opening of the bay as she took out her pencil and one of the paper labels Uncle Doran had given her. She wrote:

Sounds in the Fog
Oars breaking smooth water
Creaking of lapped boat wood
Cormorant gaining speed for flight
Mother's and Father's voices, dim and muffled by the fog
Goats—I can always hear them

In front of her, the *Doran Bull* was leaving Granger, making for open water. It became just a faded outline as it moved into the thick fog. Clem wondered that they would still set sail when the fog was so thick. In fog like this there was a danger of ships hitting rocks or other boats.

As she continued her list, she could still see her uncle

guide his sailing ship as Ray Chung raised the sails. Even though they were just a few hundred yards in front of her, the *Bull* was more and more hidden in the fog, like a fading dream. Clem added to her list:

> *The bow of the Doran Bull pushing hard and heavy against water*
> *Its sails flapping to catch the wind*
> *The distant rhythm of a paddle-wheel ship moving up the channel*

Suddenly Clem realized that the rotating paddle wheels of the steamer she heard in the channel were close by, not distant. The fog had distorted the closeness of the sound. And it was moving at full speed in the direction of Uncle Doran's boat! She hoped her uncle also heard the beating engines.

"Uncle Doran!" she shouted. "There's a steamer coming!" The wind flung her warning back, useless.

Faster than she had ever moved before, Clem began rowing after her uncle. She knew she couldn't catch him, but she hoped to get close enough for him to hear her warnings. As she entered the choppy water of the channel, she again caught a faint sight of the *Doran Bull* turning south. Right behind her uncle was the steamer. For just a second she could see both ships clearly. The steamer looked like the Border Patrol boat, the kind Officer Clark would use. Both boats then disappeared in the curtain of fog, leaving Clem unsure of what she saw. Was it the patrolmen? Or a boat that looked similar to theirs?

"Uncle Doran!" Clem tried calling again, still rowing hard.

Then she heard her uncle yell, "Tack!" The command was followed by the sound of wood moving through water, rope and canvas hitting each other in the wind. Clem stopped rowing to listen more carefully. There had been something alarming in her uncle's voice, an edge like fear.

Thickening fog closed in around Clem. She could barely distinguish the two boats. They were just brown masses in swirling clouds. Then the steamer's engines slowed and stopped.

In the new quiet she heard a man's voice, faint with distance. "We can't chance it. Get rid of them." She couldn't tell where the voice was coming from or whose it was. Muffled shuffling and shouts came from one of the boats. Clem sensed something was terribly wrong. *Is Uncle Doran in trouble?* She had to find out, she had to help. She rowed in the direction of the shouting. Suddenly she heard a loud splash and then two more. Something or someone had gone overboard. Clem knew this as soon as she heard the sound.

"Uncle Doran?" Clem screamed in panic. No one answered. The sound of the steamer's paddle wheels started up and grew distant.

Had the steamer been going after the *Doran Bull*? She remembered the patrolman questioning Uncle Doran about Ray Chung. If it was the patrol boat, were they trying to save Uncle Doran? But then why were they leaving? Why weren't they looking for a man overboard? Had Ray Chung been attacking her uncle? In her mind Clem saw her uncle and Ray Chung struggling on deck and her uncle going overboard. She scanned the water's surface. Where? Where had the splashes come from? Finally she stopped rowing and rested the oars. Failure and despair flooded through her.

As she sat, stunned, a burst of bubbles rose to the surface beside the *Fisherbird*. She leaned over the side of her boat. Something large and brown was sinking slowly. "Uncle Doran!" Clem grabbed the metal hook secured to a long pole that she used for hooking large fish. She jabbed the pole through the water as far down as she could reach, just snagging the sinking lump. The heavy mass caught hard, and Clem had to brace her legs against the boat to hold on to the end of the pole. Her grip was fragile, and Clem felt her hands grow slick with sweat. She was afraid that at any moment the pole would slide out of her hands, letting whatever it was sink into the grasping currents of deep water.

Clem pulled the pole as hard as she could, hand over hand. She heard herself grunt with muscle strain until she could raise the mass. Slowly it began to surface. More bubbles escaped, and Clem could see that whatever she held was wrapped in burlap.

As the wet fabric hit the air, Clem fell to her knees and leaned over the water to grab it. To her shock, through the rip made by the grappling hook, a hand suddenly thrust out and grabbed on to her wrist, pulling her to the very edge of the *Fisherbird*.

CHAPTER 5

Things I Have Been Afraid Of

Having to talk to people I don't know
Pirates and thieves
Entering the root cellar without a candle
All spiders except the long-legged skinny ones
Something coming out of deep dark water to get me

As Clem dropped to the bottom of the boat to keep from being pulled into the water, she remembered her list of fears. It passed through her mind like a distant flash of light.

The hand came out of a large burlap bag, the kind grain was sold in. The wet fingers dug hard into her wrist, like the roots of kelp wrapping around rock. Clem's fear clung to her whole body as hard as the hand that held her wrist. She couldn't think of anything but pulling the body out of the water. Inching slowly, Clem pulled herself to the back of the *Fisherbird*, where she could drag the sack in without tipping the dory.

With a huge breath, she heaved the load over the edge of the boat. The bow rose into the air and the stern dipped to the water's edge, threatening to swamp the *Fisherbird*. Finally she managed to pull the burlap bag in and drop it. Gasping, Clem crouched on the boat's bottom, watching the dripping sack that was tied closed with rope. It didn't move, and she was afraid the person inside was now dead or very close to death.

Was it Uncle Doran? Had Ray Chung tied him in a bag and flung him into the sea? "Look inside," she murmured to herself. But she just sat there panting and trying to calm her pounding heart. When she finally reached out and touched the bag, the hand reaching out of the torn opening quivered.

Then, suddenly, the mound at her feet convulsed, ridding itself of seawater. Clem saw the fabric strain and heave. This pushed her into action, and she ripped the soggy burlap away.

It wasn't Uncle Doran. Tears of relief heated her cheeks. Inside lay a Chinese man she had never seen before, curled over and retching.

"Are you all right?" Clem whispered, almost too low to be heard. She felt sick and sad watching him try to breathe. The man didn't answer. He continued to vomit seawater.

Clem thought, *What did he do to make someone tie him in a bag and push him over?* More important, from which boat? Was he an escaped convict from the patrol boat? Or could he have been thrown from the *Doran Bull*? *No*, Clem insisted to herself. *He didn't come from Uncle Doran's boat.*

She remembered the voice saying, "Get rid of them." Were there others, right now, sinking slowly into the brown seaweed and gravel of the sea bottom? She imagined them inside the dark bags, eyes starkly open yet unseeing. She saw the fabric rotting away under water, releasing stiff limbs lifting and swaying with the invisible currents, like marionette puppets.

"Where did you come from?" she questioned the man. "Not from the *Doran Bull*." The sound of her voice speaking out loud almost convinced her. "Uncle Doran was helping you, I'm sure of it." Only the dampness of fog answered her. The body lay still.

Maybe he was someone Ray Chung knew. Maybe he was a smuggler. Or maybe he was running away from something.

Clem remembered a conversation at the supper table when the Expulsion Act had been passed. Clem's father was satisfied with the new law. "Now no more yellow men will take jobs from Americans."

"But Daa, you're a foreigner. You're Scottish!" Clem had said.

"He means white people like us when he says Americans," Clem's mother had responded seriously. "Remember, before your Uncle Doran bought his boat, he lost a good railroad job to the Chinese. They came in and worked for wages no white man could live on."

"Doran, I don't know how you can stand having one of them on your boat," Clem's father had said.

Uncle Doran had laughed strangely. "Ray Chung's the perfect deck hand. Lets me do all the talking while he does all the hard work."

Looking down into the bottom of her boat, Clem

watched the man she had rescued groan. He seemed to be straining somewhere between unconscious and awake. She tried again to speak to him. "Are you all right?"

That was when Clem began to look around. The tide had turned, and its current was taking her boat farther into the channel. She needed to decide what to do before they were carried out too far to row back against the strong currents that came with the tide change.

She must take him home, where her mother and father could help him. Even if he was Chinese, they would help a person in need. Her father would probably flag down the patrol boat and turn the man over to the Revenuers, but not without binding his wounds and giving him food.

The man's arms and legs jerked in sudden muscle spasms. Clem straddled the curve of the *Fisherbird* and pushed the dead weight to the back so she could row. As she lifted him, his eyes opened and, like a seal caught in a fish net, he looked around in a panic of the unknown.

Seeing his face, Clem reassured him. "I'm going to get help for you. I'll take you home."

The man shook his head, the fear in his eyes contaminating his face. "No!" He forced the word from his mouth.

"No?" Clem stared at him in surprise. "But you need help. A doctor."

"No one, no one must find me," he insisted.

"Why not?" Clem leaned close to hear his words. The man's English was clear and practiced, despite being weak.

"Danger," he said in a fading voice. The strain of speaking sucked him into darkness again and he only moaned in response to her questions.

"But if I can't take you home, what will I do?" she wondered aloud. His words frightened her. Maybe the boat she had seen chasing Uncle Doran wasn't the patrol at all. She remembered that in Canada, just last year, a band of smugglers had disguised their ship to look like the Border Patrol and smuggled whiskey and opium for months without being discovered. Now she imagined the steamer was filled with criminals of some sort. And that was why Uncle Doran was trying to get away. If that was true, would the outlaws in the steamer come to her house after her family? "I can't take you home," she said.

The smell of vomit mixed with seaweed rose from the floor of her boat. Clem swallowed her own stomach upset. She suddenly was frightened of the man she had saved. He could be one of the criminal smugglers her father talked about. She almost wished the man had sunk away to the darkness instead of snagging on her pole.

The man groaned weakly. What could she do?

Then she noticed that the *Fisherbird* was drifting south, toward Spirit Island. "That's it!" she said out loud. Hardly more than a rock with a few trees growing at the center, Spirit Island was separated from the south side of Granger by a narrow passage of water. The island was uninhabited. Being only a couple of acres, it was too small to farm. People said that long ago the Lummi Indians had used it as a burial place. But her father said it wasn't true or today they would find bones and old Indian tools.

If anyone were looking for him, the Chinese man would be safely hidden on Spirit Island while she could get help from her father.

Clem knew that at the center of Spirit Island there was a large stone outcropping that could shelter the man from wind and rain. It was the safest place she could think of to take him.

Clem rowed straight and hard until she heard the gravel scrape the bottom of the *Fisherbird*. Jumping out into the cold water, Clem remembered her skirt and tucked the wet hem quickly into her belt. She leaned her weight into pulling the heavy boat high onto the shore. Then she looked around. The pocket of beach was surrounded by steep rock cliffs, about four feet higher than Clem's head. She needed both hands and feet to climb the narrow trail. How would she get the sick man above the waterline?

Clem examined the man's face. A deep cut over one eye left blood over half his face. She could see it was swelling now, and there were bruises coming out on the other side of his face as well. "You were beaten?" she asked even though she knew he couldn't respond.

Clem lifted the man like a hay bale and laid him on the beach. *He's not so big*, she thought. Standing, she knew he would be a good two inches shorter than she was. Clem took the extra rope off the dory's stern. Kneeling low beside the man, she pulled him onto her back and lashed the rope around both of their waists, their two bodies stacked like mattresses. Then she crawled to the cliff bottom.

By staying bent she could balance the body while climbing to dry earth above. Usually Clem wouldn't have noticed a scramble up the seven- or eight-foot rock. But with the man on her back, each inch felt like a huge distance. At the top she collapsed with her face in the dirt. Panting, she stared at the orange lichens that grew flat on the rocks here. Warm sun melted over the plants. They gave off a smell like that of roses and cedar boughs wrapped up together. She couldn't help wishing she could just lie there forgetting the burden she carried. For an instant she wondered if lichens had names as plants did. "Get up," Clem commanded herself.

Clem untied the rope and rolled the man off her back. Now she could wrap her arms under the man's shoulders and drag him up the slope through the salal bushes and ferns. His worn boots left two narrow troughs in the soft pine-needle peat. But he remained still and quiet. Stopping often to rest, Clem checked to make sure the man was still breathing. No longer moving and groaning, he seemed to have drifted somewhere far away where he could not feel or hear Clem.

Clem wondered if he was dying.

At the top of the island Clem laid the man gently to rest under the hanging lip of stone. She then gathered fir boughs to cover him like a quilt. His clothes were starting to dry against him, stiff like the blood in his hair. All the time he was as still as the thick tree trunks that surrounded them. Clem leaned over him listening for breath. It was shallow now, barely moving his chest.

Clem sat a few minutes, observing the unmoving form. Above her, the breeze began to sway the trees, sounding like murmured voices. *It's like the singing at Paul Hersey's funeral,* she thought. But she knew a north wind could make getting home difficult. She needed to leave.

"If you have to die, this is not a bad place to do it," Clem whispered as she headed back to the *Fisherbird*.

Clem had already rowed beyond the quarter-mile gap

between Spirit and Granger Islands when she heard the man's voice, tearing the air into fragments that slapped against her, wordless screaming over and over from the top of Spirit Island.

CHAPTER 6

Things I Have Found in the Sea

Three round glass balls that float
A perfect sea urchin shell with all its spines attached
Driftwood that looks exactly like our cow's head
Many bottles—blue are the best, red the rarest
Two old boots and one small lady's slipper
One live man

Clem tried to recite one of her lists from memory to block out the screaming that pulled at her feelings. But the noise was as strong as the horse when it was harnessed to their plow. Finally she stopped rowing to listen. What should she do? The man needed help, but if she stayed away too long she would be caught in the outgoing tide, making it hard to fight the currents home.

But then quiet settled over the water like the coming of night. Clem wondered what had happened. She turned to look behind her and saw her father two hundred yards in the distance, making his way over the rocks that edged their island. She could see him scanning the water for her. Had he heard the screams?

Clem waved in her father's direction. As soon as he saw her, he returned the greeting and turned toward home. No matter what was happening on Spirit Island, she couldn't go back now. Her father had seen her coming.

With the bailing bucket Clem rinsed as much of the mess out of the boat as she could. She sloshed salty water over the vomit then bailed it out again, using the burlap sack to wipe the wood clean. Then she took up her oars again.

Back in her own bay Clem beached the *Fisherbird*.

"I thought you were lost, Clemmy," her father said, walking down the beach to help her drag the *Fisherbird* up.

Clem looked at his face, searching for signs that her father had heard the screaming, but it was clear and easy.

"You've missed your noon meal," he continued.

"I saw a steamer," Clem started to tell her dad. Her voice took on all the shaking emotions she had been feeling. "It almost ran into the *Bull*." She ached to tell her father everything that had happened.

"Doran was a fool to start out in this weather," her father responded.

Her father helped her gather the things out of the *Fisherbird*. "What is that, Clem?" he interrupted her, pointing to the ragged burlap bag lying in the bottom.

"I found it in the water," Clem began. "From one of the boats . . ." The story was slipping out, like water she tried to cup in her hand. The man's life was more of a burden than she could bear. But before she could tell the details, she heard steps on the gravel beach behind them.

"Joseph, Clem." Uncle Doran came striding over the stones. To Clem's surprise Ray Chung was with him.

"Where did you come from?" Clem's father asked. He nodded to Ray Chung in an uncomfortable greeting. Clem knew that her father hadn't expected to see her uncle's deck hand on shore. "Where is the *Bull*?"

"We anchored on the east side of the island," Uncle Doran said.

"The east side? There's no protection there," Clem's father said.

"We stop only briefly," Uncle Doran said. "We circled the island, waiting for the fog to clear further out in the channel." Then, almost as if he were wondering out loud, "You haven't had any visitors today, by chance?"

"Visitors?" Clem's father seemed puzzled. "Who?"

Clem saw her uncle and Ray Chung exchange a look. "We thought we saw the Revenue boat cutting a close line on the island," Uncle Doran said.

"Was it really the Revenuers?" Clem asked without thinking.

"Did you see anyone out there, Clemmy?" her father asked her.

"You were outside the bay?" Uncle Doran turned to Clem. His voice rose in loudness, almost fierce.

It stopped Clem from being able to answer. All she could do was nod. Uncle Doran was afraid of something! His fear hit hard against Clem, like rowing into a cold wind. Her uncle's displeasure trapped all her words tight inside her.

In the silence Ray Chung glanced at her dory and

walked over to it. He lifted the torn piece of burlap and fingered it, holding it out for Uncle Doran to see. Then he dropped the fabric back into the boat.

"What were you doing out there?" Uncle Doran stared at her as if she were a criminal. Never had she seen such a look on his face.

"I—I was checking my crab traps," she stammered, her fear making her jaw stiff.

"What did you see?" Doran asked, his voice a slap.

"I saw a steamer in the fog, but I wasn't sure if it was the Border Patrol." Clem felt tears of fear form in her eyes. Why was her uncle so angry? "I thought they were going to hit you."

"What else? What else did you see?" Uncle Doran asked. "Where did you get that burlap?"

"Doran!" Clem's father interrupted. "What is the matter with you? Clemmy was out in her boat, that's all."

Instantly Uncle Doran's face became smooth. His voice changed back to the carefree tone that Clem knew so well. "Nothing is wrong, Joseph. It was foggy out there today. As the Revenuers found out. Not a safe day for my niece to be in the channel." He put his big hand on Clem's head. She could feel it tremble.

Then Ray Chung said, "The wind is fresh from the south. We should not leave the *Bull* where it is. She could drift."

"Right," Uncle Doran responded. "Well, Joseph, send my regards to Sarah and Fanny." He glanced at the house warily.

Clem remembered her uncle holding Sarah's hand in

his. *Maybe he's in such a foul mood because he has finally seen through Sarah's disguise to her true greedy self,* Clem tried convincing herself.

"When will we see you next?" Clem's father asked.

Uncle Doran didn't seem to hear her father. He stared at Clem for one more minute before heading up the beach.

The next morning, with the first hint of light, Clem slid out of the bed she shared with Sarah. As quietly as possible she placed her feet on each step, easing her legs downstairs. Just below her was the thin wall that separated her parents' bedroom from the main room of the house. She didn't want anyone to wake now.

The night before, Clem had decided to leave early and return to Spirit Island. There she would see if the Chinese man was alive or dead. If dead, then there would be no more danger. If he was alive, she would insist that the Chinese man answer all her questions.

Clem had told her father she would be going out early, before the wind came up, to fish for cod and reset her crab pots. Now she moved over to the food cupboard, taking bread and apples, just enough that she didn't think her mother would notice. She wrapped the food in an old flour sack rag and filled a water can from the bucket by the door.

The bay in the early dawning was smooth like the back of a silver spoon. When Clem leaned over the side of her boat, she could see long fronds of bulbous kelp floating in dancing rhythms, its roots anchored to the rocks below.

Because of high tide there was no beach exposed on Spirit Island when Clem arrived. She brought the *Fisherbird* alongside the pale sandstone cliff and tied it to a tree that grew at the island's rocky edge.

As she climbed onto the rocks of Spirit Island, the sun was a small white crescent just rising above the high point of Orcas Island farther to the northeast. Clem saw the light catch on the broad surface of a salal leaf.

Standing on the trail, she hesitated. In front of her were the firs that formed the Chinese man's shelter. What would she find? She remembered finding a dead seal on the beach the year before. Would he be stiff-limbed and starting to swell, as the round seal had been? Would the skin of his face be rising to enclose blind eyes?

"Go," Clem commanded herself, trying to force her feet to move. Finally she started up the steep trail. There he was, just as she had left him.

He is dead, Clem thought. A strange mix of feelings pumped through her like blood, sadness and relief all stirred together. She squatted down, watching. As she did she saw clearly the man's chest rise and fall with his breath. *He's alive*, she realized. Slowly Clem approached and leaned over, checking the man's face as if she were searching a deep tidal pool. His eyes were closed and still. Dried blood stained half of his face and crusted around one eye. Clem poured a little water on her hand and tried to wipe away the blood.

As she touched him the man's eyes opened. Their looks met and he screamed, sliding back from her until he was blocked, halted by the mossy boulders. Clem jumped in the opposite direction.

"I'm sorry," Clem pleaded. "I didn't mean to frighten you."

"Who are you?" the man asked, his voice raspy and weak as if it could barely escape his throat.

"I pulled you out of the water yesterday," Clem whispered. "I brought you here. Don't you remember?"

"I remember going in, but not coming out." The man slumped to one side.

Clem watched him collapse. Moving to him, she kneeled down and eased him to the ground.

"At some time, I opened my eyes to a huge darkness," he struggled to say. "I felt myself sinking. I screamed, again and again, hoping the water would fill my lungs and end my suffering. After that, I know nothing."

"I brought food," she told him.

The man refused, shaking his head. "Water?"

Clem held the water can to the man's lips, but it dribbled down his cheeks. So she slid one hand under his shoulders and lifted him to drink. Her hand molded itself around thin bones. He drank eagerly until he began to cough, spewing much of the water back out of his mouth, wetting the front of his shirt. He dropped his head back, exhausted. Still, his eyes were watching her.

"Why were you in the water?" she asked.

The man groaned, putting his hands over his stomach.

"My belly is sick, from eating the sea."

"But why? What happened? Were you on the *Doran Bull*?" With this last question Clem's voice became faint with fear of the answer.

"They told us we must hide, be still. We must be hidden inside the bags for the whole time, to look like sacks of grain."

"How many others?" Clem asked in a low voice. She imagined bodies floating like the kelp.

"Two others." Then the man went on, his voice growing stronger. "The captain said, 'They're coming, Ray Chung!'" The man's eyes stared through Clem. "I felt we must be chased by demons."

"The Revenuers," Clem told him. "They were chasing you." She saw that he understood what she was talking about. "Why?"

The man seemed to fill out with a tiny spark of renewed strength. His eyes lost the unfocused look. "My name is Tong-Ling. I am *gum shan hok*." At Clem's confused look he explained, "it means 'guest of the Golden Mountain.' I paid for passage on the captain's boat."

"Doran Nesbitt," Clem said. "The *Doran Bull*. He was helping you. How did you fall overboard?"

"No! He cared nothing for helping us. We were pushed!"

CHAPTER 7

Things I Might Learn in School

Uses for numbers other than counting
Why people look so different and yet so much the same
Why there are so many languages
Why some people do what is bad

As Clem listened to Tong-Ling's explanation, she murmured out loud, "There were others." She remembered the splashes, more than one. "But why were you hiding on the *Bull*?"

Tears filled Clem's eyes. Wonderful, boyish Uncle Doran, who loved her and always made her feel good. Could he really have done such a terrible thing? Thrown people off his boat? It was as if he were two completely different people that Clem couldn't fit together in her mind. There *must* be an explanation. She wouldn't give up on Uncle Doran yet.

Tong-Ling tried to sit up. Clem helped by pushing his shoulders into a sitting position against the cold stones.

"I am *gum shan hok*," he repeated, as if she would understand. "I paid to return." He held the water can to his mouth and was able to drink.

She saw Tong-Ling try to gather the energy to continue his story. "I was very young when I left my home in China. But others had gone before me. They had gone to dig gold. I grew up seeing the money being sent back. And despite the dishonor it did my parents, I came too. I thought the money I sent would make up for my leaving."

"Can you eat anything now?" Clem asked.

Tong-Ling took a small bite of the bread she held out to him.

Clem studied Tong-Ling's face as he tried to eat. The only place his face showed any age was around his eyes, where lines came and went as he spoke. She couldn't tell how old he might be, thirty or fifty. Part of him looked young, but then a second later she thought he must be ancient.

"At first," he said, "I had planned only to stay in this country to make enough money to return home, buy land, and take a wife. I worked hard in the gold fields and then on the railroads."

"Did you go back?" Clem asked.

Tong-Ling nodded. "I went back. But I learned that there is never enough."

Suddenly Clem heard the bushes rustle in the direction of the trail. She held her finger to her lips in warning.

Tong-Ling's face became pale and his eyes fearful. "No one must find me!" he hissed. "Or I will be dead."

Clem signaled him to crouch under a low rock overhang. Quickly she placed the blanket of fir boughs over him.

"Don't move."

Standing up, Clem glanced down the trail to see if someone was coming. She hoped it was just one of the small deer that lived in the islands. But it didn't sound like a deer browsing; it sounded like a person walking. She thought, *What if it's Uncle Doran or Ray Chung?* Uncle Doran had seen the burlap in her dory yesterday. He must have suspected that she had rescued at least one Chinese man from his boat. If he found them, what would he do? Could her uncle really kill Tong-Ling? She caught a glimpse of a blue shirt in the salal below.

The person looked up. It was Jed Parsons, the boy she had met at Paul Hersey's funeral. She was stunned and forgot to duck below the foliage lining the trail. Right away Jed saw her.

"I've been looking for you, Clem Nesbitt." He waved a skinny arm. "The tide's going out, and if you don't move that dory of yours she'll soon be hanging like a spider on its thread."

"Oh no, the *Fisherbird*!" It was still tied to the cliff. Clem had forgotten to keep track of the time. She could have slapped herself. In the islands, you always had to watch your boat. Leave it on the beach unattended for too long and you could find yourself left high and dry when the tide goes out. Or worse, the tide could come in and take your boat as quick as a thief's quiet hand.

How could I have been so stupid? she asked herself, and she started to run down the trail.

"Even from a quarter mile off, I knew that was your dory tied there," Jed said. "I thought maybe something happened that you'd leave your boat hanging like that."

As she streaked past him, Clem yelled, "Come on!"

"I guess it's not the best time for chatting," Jed said as he followed her.

At the cliff's edge Clem peered over, afraid of what she would find. The bowline extended stretch-tight down the rocks. On the end was Clem's *Fisherbird* listing to the side. Jed's smaller dinghy was tied up next to it.

"It's almost out of the water," Clem exclaimed. "We have to hurry."

"I could have told you that," Jed said.

"Help me now," Clem said, trying to be patient. "You get down in your boat and see if you can keep her from scraping the rocks as I lower the rope. Then we'll take both boats around to the cove."

Jed climbed into his small dinghy and looked back for instructions. His face was attentive. Clem felt herself relax a bit. A moment later the *Fisherbird* floated again and she was at the oars.

"I'll follow you to the cove, Captain," Jed said, saluting.

Clem recognized the honest friendliness in his voice and longed to salute back. Should she tell him about Tong-Ling? The words rose in her throat, wanting to be said. She stopped herself. *No one must find out about Tong-Ling. Not until I know what's really going on.* She knew she had to get rid of Jed.

When they had moved their boats around to the cove where the tide couldn't get them, Clem asked, "What are you doing over here?"

"I came camping," Jed answered. "'Woodzing,' my pa calls it. He said he spent a lot of time tramping the woods in

North Carolina when he was a pup. Says it'll make a man out of me."

"Why here?" Clem couldn't hide her disappointment that she had company. "Why not explore your own island?"

"I've done that plenty," Jed said. "Now that my little brothers can be a help-out on the farm, Pa lets me go for a spell and I do some tromping. I pretty much know every hole and hill that ain't under the protection of a shotgun on Lopez."

Thoughts rambled through Clem's head as Jed talked. How could she convince him to leave the island? But Jed didn't notice. He went right on talking.

"Then, last Monday, Pa traded a mess of garden stuff to George Davis for this dinghy. George doesn't have a wife. And he told Pa he was so sick of eating only codfish he'd trade his left leg for a cabbage. And that's a big trade because he only has a left leg. Lost the other one cutting logs over on Orcas."

Clem couldn't help laughing at Jed's story. She examined his flat-bottomed dinghy and thought it was awfully poor next to her graceful dory.

Jed said, "Not worth more than a few cabbages, is it? Oh, I know it's nothing next to your fine craft, but it's steady and the leaks are slow enough to give me time enough to get someplace."

Again Clem was laughing. Jed had such a funny way of talking. The way his words came out all together like a knotted string was almost like a combination of laughing and singing.

Clem's smile seemed to encourage Jed and he plowed

ahead. "I'd sure like to have you show me how to do the crabbing."

"I can't today," Clem fumbled. She tried to think of some way to get rid of him. "I'm doing a chore for my mother."

"I'll help you," Jed offered. "Ma packed me enough supper to feed half the workers at the lime quarry, so we can do your chores and then feast away."

"I don't think so," Clem grumbled nervously. "I'm looking for the wild ginger that my mother uses to make her tonic." Even as her mind tried to race ahead of Jed's thinking, Clem decided to make a list of all the plants her mother did use for cooking.

"I'll just tag along, then," Jed offered, not giving up. "Look for a place to pitch my camp. It looks like there's a nice spot up around those big trees right on top of the island."

Clem groaned as Jed pointed right in the direction of where Tong-Ling was hidden.

"I'm not going there." Clem tried to sound decisive. "The ginger grows down here."

"Maybe then I'll take a run up to check out the place," said Jed. Clem saw him gazing with longing at the hill.

"No!" Clem thought fast. "It's a graveyard up there. The natives used to lay out their dead here."

But instead of scaring Jed off, her words caused his face to shine. "Loosey in Saint Loosey! I gotta see that. I've never been to an Indian cemetery before."

"It's not right," Clem said. "The dead shouldn't be disturbed."

"Clem Nesbitt, I got the good manners my mamma taught me, and enough respect for folks to use my eyes only and leave my hands in my pockets," Jed said.

"My father said it isn't right to poke around there," Clem argued.

"But that's where you were when I found you!" Jed said, as if he was just remembering that fact himself. "I'm going. No one will see me."

Jed stepped around her and started crashing through the brush, heading for the clearing. Clem started after him in a panic.

Almost as if he knew she was looking for something to make him turn back, Jed walked faster. "Wait, Jed!" Clem called.

"I'm a-going!" Jed took the longest strides Clem had ever seen. And they weren't determined steps, but happy steps like skipping.

"My father said I was never to go there," Clem panted.

"I won't tattle on you," Jed said. And with these words he broke out of the barrier of brush and came into the circle of stones. Clem came rushing after him, expecting to see Tong-Ling and Jed staring at each other in shock.

"So where's the bodies?" Jed looked around him, disappointed.

Clem looked too. The clearing was empty. She glanced over to the cleft in the rocks. She saw the tree branches piled up just as she had left them. Tong-Ling hadn't moved in all this time.

"Well?" Jed wanted an answer.

Clem felt confident now. She thought Jed would lose

interest in a few minutes and she could lead him away. "Bodies? There hasn't been any dead left here in years. Since long before any settlers came. Only spirits left, and they're invisible, of course."

"No dead bodies." Jed's excitement dried up like a spring in a drought. "What were you doing up here?"

"I told you." Some of Clem's nervousness returned. "I was looking for my mother's tonic plant."

Jed started looking at the ground like he was searching for something. "You sure left a lot of scruffy tracks to have just meandered on up here. Looks like you spent some time."

"How do you know that?"

"This dirt is soft and holds the tracks. Look-see, here's your footprints coming off the trail, and then they are all over the area like you walked around a bunch. There's that indent where you sat a while. And something else."

Clem held her breath. "What?"

"It looks like something was dragged up here. Look at those straight lines running across the area to over there." Jed pointed right to Tong-Ling's hiding place. He started to follow the tracks.

"Wait!" Clem called out, but he had already reached out for the fir branches.

CHAPTER 8

Things I Like About Jed

Likes everyone unless forced not to
Sees people's hearts, not what they look like
Speaks his own "Jed" language
Makes me laugh
Can spit

Jed gave only a quick backward glance to Clem's pleas before pulling the bushes away from Tong-Ling's hiding place. Tong-Ling and Jed stared at each other for what felt to Clem like forever. Tong-Ling lay pressed against the rock as if he hoped it would absorb him. His short, straight hair stuck out from his head in matted spines like a sea urchin's. Clem could see the surprise on Jed's face when he found the man cowering in fear.

Jed turned to her in question. "Hey, what's going on here?"

Clem couldn't speak. She could see panic surfacing in

Tong-Ling, about to erupt. Truths and lies crowded into her head, and she wildly tried to sort out what she should tell Jed.

But he didn't wait for her explanations. Extending his hand to Tong-Ling, he said, "You must be crunched up like a shell crab in there. Let me give you a hand."

Clem let out a sigh of relief. Tong-Ling took Jed's hand and allowed himself to be pulled up. "I'm Jed Parsons, from over to Lopez Island." He pointed toward the west.

Tong-Ling swayed against Jed, not yet strong enough to stand on his own. They stood face to face, almost exactly the same size. Jed supported Tong-Ling's weight. "You look over-baked, mister. Sort of like a jellyfish on hot rocks." He gently lowered Tong-Ling back onto the ground and set him leaning against the rocks. Turning again to Clem, Jed looked for an explanation.

Tears welled up in her eyes as she started to speak. "Yesterday I pulled him out of the water. He was almost dead."

"Did you lose your boat?" Jed asked Tong-Ling.

"Not exactly," Clem answered for the man. "His name is Tong-Ling. He's from China."

"I can see that much," Jed answered, waiting for Clem to say more.

"The miss saved my life," Tong-Ling said. "I was return-ing to this country, even though it is no longer allowed. We hid in the bottom of the boat. But the government boat was after us, and the captain, he says, 'Ray Chung, get rid of them.' And he, one of my own countrymen! He drags us, beating with the wooden club until we cannot but go over."

Clem couldn't stand to see the shocked look on Jed's

face. The tears being forced out of her felt hard, as if she were choking on them. "How can you know for certain what happened? You were tied in the bag," Clem said, groping for a list of alternatives. "Maybe Ray Chung was moving you to a better hiding place. There is a wooden locker on deck where ropes are stored. I bet they were trying to put you there. And when you struggled you hit your head and fell over."

Jed whispered, "How many?"

"I was the third," Tong-Ling said. "I heard them go."

"That could have been anything falling in," Clem insisted. Neither Tong-Ling nor Jed responded to her.

"Doran Nesbitt's been smuggling Chinese? Your uncle?" Jed sat down in disbelief.

"The captain is your relation, miss?" Tong-Ling asked.

In answer she nodded. She felt foolish for sobbing out of control in front of Tong-Ling and Jed. But she couldn't stop. "There has to be a reason," she cried. "Uncle Doran wouldn't hurt anyone! I don't believe it!" But then the memory of Uncle Doran's reaction when Ray Chung showed him the burlap in her boat came slipping under her skin.

"I am sorry I have brought you grief," Tong-Ling said. "We all wear many different faces. I see you did not know this one of your uncle's."

"I don't know it yet," Clem insisted. "I'll wait and see." But in what Tong-Ling said, Clem heard a new truth. And she immediately started making a list about Uncle Doran and Sarah. *Uncle Doran: kind but horrible? Loving but evil? I don't know anymore. Sarah: many-faced.*

Finally Jed asked Clem, "What are you going to do?"

"We have to tell someone," Clem said. She thought of

her father.

"No!" Tong-Ling shouted with newfound strength. "No one, no one must know."

"But you can't just stay here forever," Clem said.

"They will send me back," Tong-Ling said more calmly.

"If it is illegal for you to stay," Clem agreed, "then maybe you should go."

Suddenly Tong-Ling sounded angry. "For almost twenty years I work in this country. I work hard. I learn the language. I am no different from others who come. But because I am Chinese, I am hated."

Clem thought of her own family. They had not been here as long as Tong-Ling. What if it were the Scots who were being chased out? She couldn't imagine being forced to leave their island farm. But then, her father said the Chinese stole jobs from others.

"Along the coast," Tong-Ling said, "there are the fish canneries that will still hire Chinese to work along with the Indians." Almost as if he could read Clem's thoughts, he added, "It is work white people do not want. That is where I was going. First to the town of Whatcom and then north until I find work." His voice sounded as if he were asking for something.

Clem didn't know what to say. It was like yesterday when she tried to see through the fog in the channel. She knew everything was right in front of her, but she just didn't know where. Jed and Tong-Ling both seemed to be waiting for her to say something.

"I'll take you," Jed spoke out, determination swelling his voice. "I'll take you to Whatcom, or Anacortes, any town you want. We can leave right now." He shot Clem a look that made her feel terrible. And it also made her angry, as if she should simply believe the worst of Uncle Doran, without even looking for the truth.

"It's two days to Whatcom if you have wind and three hard days of rowing otherwise," she said, realizing they needed her boat and her sailing experience. "You'd never make it in that floating stump you call a boat."

"Clem Nesbitt, you can't just hand him over to be sent back to where he don't want to be. Or worse, bonked on the beam and tossed to the tide. It ain't right," Jed insisted.

"I don't believe my uncle did it," Clem screamed at Jed. "It's a mistake!" Clem broke down crying again and sat down in the dirt, hiding her eyes in her skirt.

She felt Jed come and sit by her as if he wanted to comfort her, and she tried to gain control of herself. Tong-Ling looked tired and frightened. He sat holding his head between shaking hands. She realized that his life might depend on her. "I can't believe it of Uncle Doran, I just can't," she managed to mumble between sobs and hiccups.

Jed moved in close and spoke softly against her ear. "I ain't known you very long, but I got the feeling that you are a pretty good person inside where the tally is kept."

"I'm not," Clem said, thinking of how she could be rude to Sarah. She swallowed new tears before they could push out of her.

"My ma always said I could sniff out fine folks just like my pa," Jed said. "It seems to run in the family. And I know I've wanted to be friends with you since I first seen ya. I don't know as a Parsons ever sniffs wrong."

Clem smiled through her swelling eyes and running nose. It was hard to avoid being friends with Jed. "We should get more food and some clothes for you," Clem said to Tong-Ling. "You can't go anywhere for two or three days. At least until you're strong again."

"Does that mean you'll be helping?" Jed asked Clem.

"I'll do what I can." Clem was still unsure what was the right thing to do.

"Yee-hah! This is going to be a real adventure," Jed exclaimed, jumping to his feet. "It's as good as rabbit stew on a plumb empty stomach! We're heading for the mainland!"

"Wait, Jed." Clem held up her hands. "I didn't say anything about going. My father would never let me take the *Fisherbird* and go away for days at a time."

"There's no need for you to go anywhere." Jed flung his arms out as if he were embracing his own idea. "While Tong-Ling's bucking up his strength, you teach me to sail. Then I'll borrow the Hinkles' sailing dory. They're always saying I can. Your pappy will never know a thing."

Tong-Ling smiled and Clem saw some color in his face for the first time. "Thank you, miss," he said. "Yesterday I barely clung to the rocks that edge death; now I can feel a steady place to put my feet."

"You'll have to let me think about it," Clem said warily. She felt as if her feet were stuck in wet beach mud and she was getting sucked in. To change the subject she again offered Tong-Ling more food.

Tong-Ling held up his hand. "Water only for now."

Jed took the can to him and helped him drink. Tong-Ling could swallow the water easily; it no longer ran down his chin.

"Clothes," Clem said, looking over his torn and soiled clothes, now dried stiff against his body. "He needs something to change into."

"I got a change in my sack," Jed chimed in. "Ma always packs extra for me. She says I've never been within a half a mile of water without falling in, and now that we're living on an island, I better have plenty of extra duds." He turned to Tong-Ling. "I'd say we fill about the same amount of space." Jed began rummaging through his wood-framed pack. He brought out pants and a cotton shirt and handed them to Tong-Ling.

Clem noticed the wind getting strong. "I need to be getting back. I'll bring back some supplies tomorrow. We'll work on you feeling better first and then decide what is right to do."

"I will give my mind to waiting," Tong-Ling said.

To Clem he really did look hopeful for the first time. Clem could only nod to Tong-Ling through the cloud of everything she was feeling. She turned and headed to the *Fisherbird*.

Rowing back with the starched wind, Clem tried to breathe deep and clear her mind. She had never before lied to her parents. There had never been an occasion to. *Is it lying to not say anything? Yes*, she thought. *And it is stealing to take the food from our kitchen.* Could she manage to keep Tong-Ling hidden for three or four days, maybe even longer? She was afraid that if her father looked at her just once in suspicion the whole story would come sliding out.

I have to think of this like any other job, she thought, trying to encourage herself. *It's like when one of the goats got cut on the rocks and I had to carry her home. I used every bit of strength I had, but I did it without help. I will be just as strong now.*

She remembered everything Tong-Ling had told her and knew what he said was true. He wasn't taking jobs from whites, and he was right about the canneries; Uncle Doran had told her it was the worst work imaginable.

The beach in Nesbitt Bay was empty as Clem secured her boat. Smoke rose from the chimney of the house. *They'll ask me where I've been,* she thought, running up the beach. She paused at the door to catch her breath and calm herself. From inside she heard her father's angry voice.

"What can Doran mean by this? She's only a child!" he yelled.

Clem couldn't remember her father ever sounding so angry before. Her knees collapsed under her with fear. She grabbed the door frame to keep herself standing. *They already know I found Tong-Ling! What did Uncle Doran tell them?* She shivered with sudden cold as if she stood in an ice-filled winter fog.

Her mother's voice sounded tight when she said, "It's not for us to decide, Joseph. Sarah isn't our daughter. I've known other girls who married at fifteen."

They aren't talking about me, Clem realized. Her shaking continued, but she felt the fear lose its grip.

"I thought I knew my own brother better than this," Clem's father stormed on.

"Calm yourself," her mother said. "I am sure this is why neither Sarah or Doran told us before today. But there is nothing we can do. She expects him by dawn and they will leave for San Francisco tomorrow. Although I don't see what the rush is all about."

Then Clem understood. Sarah was going to marry her uncle Doran. "Ugh!" she cried out in shock at the idea of her uncle and Sarah as man and wife.

Sarah and Uncle Doran, man and wife
Arms entwined
Lips touching

The list that formed in Clem's mind sickened her. She ran along the trail to the east field while trying to block out the thoughts. But they came pouring out with her tears as she forced her legs to run. Finally at the crest of the path, where the trees stood thickest, she stopped, flinging herself against a large fir trunk for support. Her stomach heaved with hurt so deep she could feel it grab her muscles all the way down to her feet. "How can he?" she pleaded to the dark tree bark and to the stiff branches above her head. She wished the tree would come alive, large and strong like her uncle. She wanted to feel its limbs, like arms, hold her and comfort her. *Tong-Ling was right; we all wear many faces. And here is yet another face my uncle wears,* Clem thought. In her mind she saw him holding hideous masks to his face one after the other.

"He couldn't, wouldn't . . ."

Before she could finish the sentence a hand grabbed her arm and wrenched her hard around. Ray Chung was sneering angrily at her.

CHAPTER 9

Things I Will Remember to Watch out for in the Future

Rotten clams
Slippery rock ledges
Swift outgoing tides
Poison, seen and unseen
All people who have a gaping black hole
where their heart should be

Clem's list raced in rhythm to her heartbeats. She could feel it knock against her ribs. But everything else was silent, as if the world held its breath with her and waited for Ray Chung to say something. The trees did not creak or whisper. She could not hear the wind move the grass or the hum of the sea in the distance.

Ray Chung gripped her arms harder until she felt bruises begin to form. "Where did you get that bag?" he asked. "The one I saw in your boat." His wide face didn't really seem to be questioning her, though. It was as if he already knew everything. He was no taller than Clem but had a broad, strong body with huge arms and shoulders from years of working sails and rigging.

"I—I found it floating in our bay," Clem stammered. Her voice was small and distant, like a faint star. She knew Ray Chung did not believe her.

Still holding her, Ray Chung said, "You were out there. You pulled one of them from the water."

He knows, Clem realized as he raged at her. Clem looked for words, anything that would make Ray Chung go away. Fear set her to shaking, but she also realized there was no longer any point in denying that she had pulled a body out of the sea. But she could do her best to mislead him.

"Tell me," he repeated. His voice was a threat as surely as if he held a gun to her head.

"I did pull a man out of the water," Clem answered slowly. She felt a strange calm take over as her mind filled with a list of ways she could keep Ray Chung from suspecting the truth. She closed her hands into tight fists, forcing herself to continue. "But he was dead. Drowned! I became frantic and threw the body back in."

Ray Chung kept staring at her. Clem thought he was looking for the truth in her face. She tried to return his look without faltering.

"It's easy enough to search the island before we leave," he said.

Finally she let a single word fall into the air between them. "Why?"

Ray Chung took a step back, letting go of Clem's arms.

Clem saw that her question surprised him. And it made her stronger. "Why did Uncle Doran do it?" She felt her voice growing louder. "People tied into flour sacks and dumped in the ocean," Clem stated. And as she thought about the Chinese men being pushed overboard, she suddenly remembered Paul, Sarah's father. What was it Officer Clark had said? His head had been crushed. Could her uncle and Ray Chung have killed him too? Why? Clem felt a tide of grief and terror surge through her.

"These Chinese know the dangers. And they pay up front," Ray Chung said, shrugging. "There's no money in selling garden seed and sewing needles to dirt-poor farmers."

"They pay to ride with you, and you throw them overboard?" Clem asked. "People from your own country?" Clem let the shock creep into her question. As she did, she inched slightly backward. Ray Chung stood between her and the trail leading back to the house.

"My country?" He sneered again. "You Europeans are all the same. I, like you, was born in America."

Clem was embarrassed. She never even considered a Chinese man as an American. Now she realized he spoke without an accent, as she did. Her own father sounded less American than Ray Chung.

A small silence settled around them. Clem knew this was the time to push past Ray Chung and try to run back to the safety of the house. She hoped she could catch him by surprise. That might give her enough time to get away.

Then she heard her father calling to her from the house. "Clemmy!"

Ray Chung looked over his shoulder in sudden panic

and grasped her arm again, drawing her close. "Not a word to anyone," he hissed into her ear. Clem tried to pull away from him and escape to her father. "You say one word and you'll find yourself, along with your parents, tied up in a bag and made to swim."

Clem didn't know if Ray Chung let go or if she jerked free, but she was running as fast as she could, up to the crest of the hill and down the other side. She saw the back of the house and her father starting up the trail. She threw herself against him with her arms locked around his neck, shaking as if with deadly cold.

"Clemmy, Clemmy." Her father returned her embrace. "Your mother and I heard you shout at the door, and saw you run past the window. I know this upsets you as much as it does us. But I'll talk to him and to Sarah when he comes tomorrow. 'Tis a lonely man's folly. That's all."

That's not all! Clem thought. She sobbed tears as salty as the bay's. She knew her father thought she was upset because Uncle Doran was going to take Sarah with him. To Clem, nothing about Sarah mattered anymore. She cried because the uncle she had loved her whole life was not who she had thought he was. He was a monster, something dark and rotting, but who was still able to make them love him and believe in him. And she couldn't tell her parents the truth. She knew Ray Chung's threat was real. One word now to her father and they would be the ones tied into grain sacks and tossed overboard.

With his arm around her, Clem's father led her back to the house, where her mother waited.

"Clementine," her mother said. "We're sorry about

Uncle Doran and Sarah too. Such a strange and sudden plan to marry." She looked at Clem with concern and then glanced over to where Sarah sat stiff and straight at the table, pretending to work on her crocheted lace. Clem saw her toss a small smug smile in her direction.

Her father delivered Clem to her mother's comfort and hot tea. Purposely turning away from Sarah, he left for outside. It was almost as if he couldn't stand to be in the same room with Sarah. Now it was Clem's turn to feel a tiny victory.

But Clem felt too shaky and drained to risk saying anything to Sarah. And she was too frightened to tell anyone the truth. Because of Ray Chung she knew that the *Doran Bull* was in the area, hovering somewhere around the island, as sure as a storm on the horizon.

Over the next hour, as Clem reflected on her run-in with Ray Chung, she was sure that he suspected she was lying. And she knew that Ray Chung intended to make sure Uncle Doran didn't leave any evidence behind. What if Uncle Doran or Ray Chung decided to search all the nearby islands? They might see smoke coming from Spirit Island.

Jed and Tong-Ling were in danger. She had to warn them. While a plan formed in her mind, she found a renewed strength stretching through her arms and legs. Her thoughts filled every space inside her, so she didn't have room for thinking of Sarah marrying her uncle. She ignored the girl for the rest of the evening.

Clem waited until everyone had gone to bed and she heard the soft breathing of Sarah's deep sleep beside her. Slowly and carefully she eased out of bed and grabbed the warm clothes she had purposely left out. Then with the greatest care she started down the stairs, trying to be as light as possible. At the bottom she stopped and listened. Nothing stirred. Clem could hear her own heart beating, and she found she was holding her breath.

With just the light of the cold moon shining into the house, Clem gathered supplies. She found two old blankets and spread them out on the table. First she took some matches. Next she went to the cupboard and found the loaves of bread her mother had baked that day. She wrapped a large piece of yellow cheese. Then she pulled open the trapdoor cut into the floor that led to the cellar. She lighted a candle stub from the coals in the stove and descended. In the cool darkness she packed apples and carrots from the bins. Back upstairs, Clem blew out the candle and began to lower the trapdoor.

Suddenly the metal ring handle slipped from her grasp, and the door banged shut. Clem froze. In the next room she heard her father stir and grumble in bed. Clem didn't dare move until she was sure all was settled again.

Clem started for the door. Just as her hand touched the latch she heard a noise from the bottom of the stairs. "And just where are you going, Clem Nesbitt?"

Clem spun around and there was Sarah, her hands on her hips as if she was about to confront her. Surely Sarah's voice would wake up her parents. Clem was frantic. She couldn't think what to do. Finally she held her finger to her lips and motioned for Sarah to follow her. Clem heard Sarah sigh with exasperation, but to Clem's relief Sarah followed her out into the night.

The moonlight lay puddled on the calm bay like a patch of silver ice. Clem looked longingly toward the *Fisherbird*, waiting to be launched from the stony beach.

"Tell me, Clem, what are you doing?" Sarah's face, even in the shadows, clearly showed her impatience.

"Nothing." Clem led Sarah as far away from the house as she dared as she tried to put together a story. "I couldn't sleep thinking about Uncle Doran wanting to marry you. So I was going out rowing."

"Why shouldn't Doran want to marry me?" Sarah said. "I am everything a prosperous man would want in a wife."

"You're too young. Uncle Doran could be your father." Clem kept them walking in the direction of the beach. If Sarah pushed too far, she thought, she would just run and jump into her boat. Sarah would never try to follow her.

"I don't care that he is old and as ugly as everyone else in your family." Sarah suddenly sounded harsh. "He's rich and has promised to give me everything I want. Besides, I know you're running away. I was watching you from the top of the stairs. You have enough food in there for a week."

Her confidence struck at Clem. Sarah was enjoying every minute of Clem's discomfort. Sarah must have been watching her for a while. Sarah had had time to pull on a dress over her nightgown. A blanket was wrapped around her shoulders.

Clem became angry. What would Sarah think if she knew just how Uncle Doran made his money? She wouldn't be so confident if she were aware that right now he was wanted by the law and could go to jail. She wouldn't be so superior if she knew the man she was about to run off with might have had something to do with her own father's death.

Clem opened her mouth to spit out all her knowledge, but she stopped. She would wait. There was a good chance that Sarah wouldn't believe what Clem said. She'd go running off to her parents or Uncle Doran himself. No, Clem needed a weapon that would keep Sarah quiet long enough to give them time to get Tong-Ling away. Instead, Clem turned to Sarah and asked her, "Do you think Uncle Doran is going to be happy to hear that you think he's ugly?" By this time Clem had led Sarah down to the beach. The tide was well in, so Clem knew it would be a few short steps and a single shove to launch her boat.

"He'll never know," Sarah said, but in her eyes Clem saw an uncertainty. "Tomorrow he comes at dawn and we're leaving right away."

"He's already here." Clem took advantage of her knowledge. "I may just run into the *Bull* out there now. I may be going on purpose to find him."

"I don't believe you." Sarah's voice rose in fear. "And I'm calling for your mother." She turned with determination.

Clem reached for anything she could to stop her. "I'll show you." Clem couldn't think beyond keeping Sarah from sounding the alarm. "Come with me."

Sarah hesitated, undecided. She looked several times between the house and the dory.

"Or go wake up my parents. I'll be to the mouth of the bay by the time you reach the house. Who knows what I'll say to Uncle Doran." Clem hoped Sarah couldn't see her trembling.

With a flounce of her head Sarah marched to the boat

and climbed in. She sat staring straight ahead while Clem quickly launched the dory. She rowed silently. It wasn't until they were in sight of Spirit Island that Sarah suddenly looked around and asked, "I don't see the *Bull*. Where are you taking me?"

CHAPTER 10

Places to Hide

In sandstone caves
With the rabbits under salal brush
Buried under piles of driftwood at the top of the beach
Behind a blank face
In quiet

Clem didn't answer Sarah. She rowed through the calm water, so dark and shiny that it looked like polished pewter. Purposely Clem steered away from the path of moonlight and stayed close to the shadowed shelter of the rocks. She even tried to hush her oars, knowing that with no wind to claim it, sound would sit on the water for anyone to collect, including her uncle Doran and Ray Chung. She scanned the darkness for a sign of the *Doran Bull*. Despite what she had told Sarah, it was the last thing she wanted to see.

Clem had Sarah safe for the moment, but what was she supposed to do with her now? She couldn't let her go back.

Sarah would run straight to her parents and Uncle Doran.

"Where are you taking me?" Sarah repeated her question. "I don't see Doran's ship."

Clem could hear Sarah's voice grow and multiply as the water and shoreline tossed her words back and forth like a ball.

A small splash of water, also magnified by the calm, caused Clem and Sarah both to startle. Behind their boat a seal's curious head peered at them. Then, as if scolding, the animal flipped its tail, slapped the water, and disappeared.

Maybe she should beach the dory and leave Sarah at the far end of Granger, Clem thought. But she would scream, and there was a good chance Sarah would be heard and discovered before Clem could get Tong-Ling away. No, she would have to take Sarah with them. She was the last person in the world Clem wanted to have along, but it was her only choice. She steeled herself against her feelings.

As softly as possible Clem said, "I'm going around the south side of the island to see if Uncle Doran is anchored there. On a calm night like this he could safely put the *Bull* anywhere."

It seemed to satisfy Sarah, as she sat quietly again. When they reached the channel between Granger and Spirit Islands and she could see the water beyond the island, Clem said, "it doesn't look like he's anchored here, so I'll tie up at Spirit Island and climb the hill. You can get a good view of the whole area from there. We'll find him." Clem shivered at the almost-truth of her words. *More likely he'll find us*, she told herself.

"You better not be lying to me, Clem," Sarah huffed.

But the farther away from Granger they got, the less afraid Clem was of Sarah. "And what are you going to do?" Clem asked the girl boldly. "Tell Uncle Doran that I pirated you away?"

"Perhaps," Sarah returned.

"And how are you going to do that? Swim?" Clem had the satisfaction of seeing Sarah look around her in panic.

"You're going to leave me on that island, aren't you?" Sarah asked in a voice that was almost a whimper.

Clem didn't say anything to reassure Sarah, but she thought this was the first time since Sarah had come to them that she sounded like she was saying what she truly felt.

As soon as the boat nudged against the rocks, Clem heard a whistle from the dark bushes. "Is that you, Jed?" Clem asked.

Jed's shaggy head popped up. "It's supposed to sound like an owl calling. Who's that with you?" Before Clem could say anything, Jed recognized Sarah; his eyes grew big and his mouth formed an O. "Hello, Sarah Hersey," he said shyly. Then he looked at her with a silly grin spread over his face like honey. "I'm real sorry about your pa. I was at the funeral."

"I remember you," Sarah said in return. "What is going on? You have to help me, Jed. Clem's going to leave me here."

"Why, she wouldn't hurt you, Sarah Hersey." Jed stepped forward to help Sarah out of the boat.

Clem rolled her eyes at Jed's reaction to Sarah. *Even he becomes melted mush around Sarah,* she thought.

"Then why am I being kidnapped? Doran won't allow this. He'll find me. Doran has promised me a fine house in

San Francisco," Sarah said to Clem. "I'll have ice cream every day and never eat fish again."

Clem ignored Sarah's whining and said to Jed, "We have to go now. We must get Tong-Ling to the mainland. Uncle Doran was planning on skipping out in the morning, but I think Ray Chung is going to come looking for Tong-Ling. He tried to get me to admit I knew something about Tong-Ling and the other Chinese."

"We aren't ready." Jed started to look scared. "Tong-Ling hasn't had time to get his legs back under him. And I don't have a sniff of know-how when it comes to sailing a boat clear over to Whatcom."

"Who is Tong-Ling?" Sarah asked. "Who's going to Whatcom?"

"I know," Clem responded, ignoring Sarah. "But there's no time to wait. I guess I'll have to sail the *Fisherbird*."

"You'll come with us?" Jed's voice filled with hope and excitement.

"What about me?" Sarah demanded. "Someone has to take me back."

"There's no other choice," Clem said, ignoring Sarah again.

"What about Tong-Ling?" Jed asked.

"It's better to take him weak than dead," Clem said. "We should go now."

"I knew you'd do right." Jed shook her hand hard. "We're partners, you and me."

"But what about me? And who is Tong-Ling?" Sarah's voice was becoming louder.

"You'll see," Clem told her as Jed rushed up the hill to

fetch Tong-Ling. Now that she had decided that she must take Tong-Ling to Whatcom herself, she blocked everything else out of her mind. She couldn't think about what to do with Sarah, or how worried her parents would be when they found her gone.

Fifteen minutes later Jed assisted Tong-Ling down the trail and into the boat. Clem could see that even in the few hours she had been gone, Tong-Ling had gotten stronger.

Clem began rowing away from Spirit Island, heading the *Fisherbird* for the mainland.

"You take me back to your parents' house right now," Sarah said desperately. She tried to ignore the Chinese man, who now stared at her curiously.

"Miss Sarah Hersey," Jed said, "this is Mr. Tong-Ling. He's from China."

Tong-Ling nodded a greeting, but Sarah ignored both Tong-Ling and Jed. Her eyes scanned the dark water for the *Doran Bull*.

Clem also looked for the boat, afraid that at any minute the *Doran Bull* would sail around the tip of one of the islands into view like a ghost rising from the grave. "If I do take you back, Sarah, how will I know you won't signal Uncle Doran and tell him we have Tong-Ling?" Clem didn't want Sarah with them, but she knew the safest place for Sarah was where Clem could see her.

"I don't care who this man is." Sarah pointed to Tong-Ling. "You either take me to Doran or take me back to Granger."

They reached the southern tip of Granger Island and slipped around the end. Clem stopped rowing, resting her arms against her knees.

"I think we should leave Sarah on your folks' island," Jed said gently to Clem. "We'll still have time to get away."

"Thank you, Jed." Sarah played with each word on her tongue and with her eyes. "Thank you for being a gentleman and looking out for me."

Clem almost agreed. But as she started to turn the dory around, a small swell of water lifted the boat slightly, letting Clem catch a glimpse of the top of a sail between the two islands. "I see the *Bull*'s mast! It's coming this way!" Without another word Clem reversed her actions and took to rowing fast.

"Where? Where is it?" Sarah stood up, looking around for the schooner.

"Sit down," Clem hissed. "You'll tip us over."

Instead, Sarah began shouting and waving her arms. "Here, over here." The *Fisherbird* rocked back and forth, its gunnels coming closer to the water.

Tong-Ling sat up from where he was resting in the bottom of the boat. "What is it?" His face took on a look of fear, with his dry lips pulled back in a grimace.

"Stop!" Clem clawed at Sarah's dress, trying to make her sit down. "You're going to send us all into the water."

But Sarah just slapped her hands away and continued to yell. The boat swayed from side to side until water sloshed over one oarlock.

Clem tried frantically to think. She had to steady the hysterical girl or she would cause them to capsize. But before she could stand, Jed closed his two hands gently around Sarah's wrist as if he were holding a small bird. "They can't see you," he almost whispered. "Sit down."

To Clem's amazement Sarah stopped screaming and looked down at Jed's pleading face. Gazing back at Granger Island as it faded into dark distance, Sarah sat down.

Heading away from the island farm, Clem kept up her fastest rowing pace. The *Fisherbird*'s wake spread out behind them like fingers reaching for home. Then as they cleared the channel Clem caught another glimpse of the *Doran Bull* in the moonlight, the distance between them making it look like a small toy. The *Bull* was sailing around Spirit Island.

"Do you think they will come looking for us?" Tong-Ling asked as he kept his eyes on the fading ship.

Shaking her head, Clem answered, "Uncle Doran can't know where we're heading. We might be going to any number of towns: Port Townsend, Victoria, anyplace. And he isn't going to stay around after it gets light, not with the Revenuers looking for him."

Darkness ate the *Bull* as they watched, and Clem thought that it was as if death had taken her uncle away. *I can't change what has happened*, she told herself.

"I'll row now," Jed said finally. "Your arms must feel like they're trying to keep our mule, Juny, to the plow when she knows it to be suppertime." Clem gratefully agreed, and they traded places.

As they did, Sarah finally looked over at Clem. "Why are you doing this to me? All I wanted was a nice life. Beautiful things to wear. Everything my father intended for me."

"Sarah," Clem explained, trying to reason with her, "Uncle Doran has been bringing Chinese workers into the country from Canada. Then when the Border Patrol chased the *Bull*, he threw them overboard. Tong-Ling is one of them."

"Why would he do that?" she asked.

"For the money. The money to buy all those things he was promising you," Clem said. "And there were other Chinese that didn't survive."

Hearing only what she wanted to, Sarah pointed at Tong-Ling. "You're the criminal. You shouldn't be here at all."

"That may be true," Clem agreed. "But he shouldn't be killed for it."

"I'm figuring it's the law that's wrong myself," Jed put in tentatively, inching his way between Clem and Sarah. Both girls glared at him.

Tong-Ling's tired eyes looked thoughtfully at Sarah. He ran his hand over the side of the boat, letting the water skim through his weak fingers. "I am no different from you," he finally said, pointing at her. "I want my belly full, but I also want more. I want a life that is of my own choosing."

"You are different from us," Clem put in, "because this is our country."

"That's right," Sarah agreed.

"By your saying only," Tong-Ling said. "If I were coming now from Europe, from a white country, I would be welcomed."

"I think he's right," Jed said. "We all came from some other place. Everyone except the Indians. They're the ones who were here first. It must be their country."

"Oh, no," Sarah insisted. "The country belongs to the people who build and plow it. Civilized people."

Now Tong-Ling sounded very angry. "Civilized? China has been a great nation for thousands of years. If you went there, you would be called a ghost or a barbarian and spat on."

"So then we are the same when it comes to our feelings about our countries," Clem said.

Tong-Ling had no answer.

Clem, Jed, and Sarah also fell silent. Jed rowed, but more slowly.

Finally Tong-Ling asked, "How long will it take us to get to the mainland, to Whatcom?"

"If there is good wind," Clem said, studying the water, "two days. If we have to row, three, maybe more." Then she pointed out the landmarks. "That's Shaw Island on our right and this big one to the left is Orcas. Beyond Orcas is more open water that we have to cross to get to the mainland and Whatcom town."

"What time do you think it is now?" Jed asked.

"After midnight," Clem answered. "I think we should keep going as long as possible and then find a place to beach the dory and sleep. By tomorrow I don't think we'll have to worry about my uncle finding us."

"It's a good thing we left when we did," Jed said looking back to where the *Bull* had been circling Spirit Island. The tiny island was now so far away that it merged, invisible, with the low rise of the other islands behind it. "You don't think they could have seen us, do you?" he asked.

Shaking her head, Clem said, "Once we get closer to Orcas we can try putting the sail up. For right now, though, there is a possibility they could still spot a white sail." Clem remembered how many times from her bedroom window she had seen a ship's sail catch the light from the moon.

"Doran will find me," Sarah said under her breath. To Clem it sounded like a prayer. One that could too easily be granted.

When they reached the western point of Orcas, the wind strengthened. Now Clem could no longer see Spirit or Granger Islands, and she felt safer.

"Jed, help me with the sail," she said.

Clem showed him how to feed the rings sewed onto the stiff edge of the sail through the line while she pulled the rope that lifted the fabric up the mast. Right away wind billowed against the canvas and pushed them forward. When Clem dropped the keel, the *Fisherbird* heeled over like a bird bending with the wind.

The quiet swish of water sliding against the planks sent a spark of thrill through Clem, as it always did. Sailing made her feel joined to the breeze, as graceful and light as the invisible air. They were moving fast, which exposed them more to the cold wind.

As they began to move with the breeze, Clem thought of a wind list in her mind.

Empty calm (another place to hide in)
Light air that tickles
Moderate breeze, perfect for moving my boat
Strong breeze to challenge my arms and brain
Any gale, turn around and run for home

Tong-Ling began to shiver, his teeth chattering loudly. Clem passed a blanket to him and Jed helped wrap it around his body, crouched in the bottom of the boat. Clem stayed in the very stern of the boat in order to steer with the rudder. "Sarah, you need to sit on the high side of the boat next to Jed. That will counterbalance it."

With no argument Sarah slid over to Jed, her own blanket pulled tight around her. As if she had completely forgotten how she had screamed for the *Bull*, she now cuddled close to him, saying, "You'll keep me warm, won't you, Jed?"

"Yes, miss," Jed responded.

Clem tried not to stare at them and pretended not to care. She soon felt herself start to shiver and wondered how far they could make it tonight before they were too cold and tired to keep sailing. Tong-Ling was still weak, and a night of cold could be too much for him. She found herself straining to see the shoreline of Orcas Island on their left and trying to remember just where the farms dotted the shore and where it was still uninhabited. She wanted someplace well hidden from a passing boat.

As on the other islands, most of the trees on Orcas had been cut down and sold for lumber or fuel for steamships. Only where the land rose in steep cliffs from the water was there forest left. In these places the trees often grew to the waterline and hung over the rocky beaches, making cavelike hiding spots that stayed dark even at noon. That was what Clem looked for now.

After several hours of following the shore of Orcas, Clem could no longer feel her fingers where they clutched the rudder. Her shivering came in waves of sleepiness and she knew she must rest. Tong-Ling lay quiet under the blanket, moving only if she had to tack, changing the boat's direction.

Sarah hunched close to Jed, her head drooping in exhaustion.

Clem saw a forested place along the shore and turned the boat toward it. Soon they were out of the wind and the sail fluttered loosely. She let it drop, raised the centerboard, and started rowing.

As she rowed to shore, Clem tried to plan the remainder of the trip. They would sleep tonight. Then tomorrow they must stick close to the shore of Orcas all the way to the far eastern side. From there they must head across the wide channel to Whatcom.

Jed roused himself out of a cold stupor. "What are we doing?"

"We need to rest," Clem answered. "If we pull the boat up under the trees, I don't think it'll be seen."

He nodded, and when the boat scraped bottom he jumped out to pull it in. It was a perfect spot where neither the boat nor even a small campfire could be spotted through the dense cover of trees and bushes.

Clem reached down to Tong-Ling. "We're stopping to rest." She gently shook his shoulder. Tong-Ling looked bleary-eyed. Both Jed and Clem, each supporting an arm, tried to help him ashore.

"No need," Tong-Ling insisted. "I am strong now." Clem was happy to see him able to hop out of the *Fisherbird* and onto the beach himself, even though he immediately sat down on a log to rest.

"And what about me?" Sarah demanded from the boat.

Clem felt drained and wondered how Sarah could even summon the energy to speak, let alone be so sharp tongued. But Jed went directly to her and held out his arms to help her out of the boat.

Clem found a flat spot just a few feet from the beach and helped Tong-Ling to lie down. It was damp under the trees. "Jed, we need a fire right away. I'm afraid Tong-Ling is very cold."

"I'm starving," Sarah announced. "Isn't there anything to eat? And you don't really expect me to sleep in the dirt?"

Tossing Jed's pack hard at Sarah so that she had to jump back out of the way, Clem said, "Here, make sure you divide everything four ways. And remember this has to last until we get Tong-Ling to Whatcom."

"Don't you worry," Jed rushed to reassure Sarah. "I know how to make you the warmest, softest bed you ever slept on yet. I'll be at it as soon as we scrape together this fire."

Clem and Jed gathered brush and sticks as quickly as they could. "This wood is slick-darn clammy," Jed said, looking at his six matches. "I only packed a few."

"I have a few, but we need something good for tinder." Clem looked around her. She thought of tearing a piece of her petticoat, but it was wet from unloading the dory. Then she saw Sarah sitting on a log unpacking the food and carefully tearing four pieces of bread off the loaf. As she began eating a chunk of bread, Clem went to her, bent down, and grabbed the hem of Sarah's skirt.

"Hey! What are you doing?" Sarah tried to gather the nice fabric into her hands protectively.

"We need fire starter." Clem ripped.

"Not off my dress!"

"You're here eating our food," Clem told her. "You

might as well be good for something."

"We're thanking you for your contribution, Miss Sarah." Jed smiled at the girl.

"Miss Sarah," Clem mimicked him, making sure she was loud enough for everyone to hear.

Sarah stomped her foot and took another bite of bread. "This is dry without any butter," she complained.

"If you don't like it, stop eating so much and give some to Tong-Ling," Clem told her.

"Here." With resentfulness, Sarah handed Tong-Ling a piece.

Clem spread her rubber throw-over on the ground and sat down near the fire Jed had started. She could barely keep her eyes open as she tried to eat her piece of dry bread. Jed was making a bed for Sarah as if she were some kind of royalty.

Tomorrow, since we don't have to worry about Uncle Doran, Clem thought, *I'll set the fishing line and catch us a real dinner. And I bet Princess Sarah won't turn up her nose at a codfish then.*

CHAPTER 11

Things I Know to Be True

Uncle Doran has broken my heart.
I am hurting my parents by leaving.
I never want to be like Sarah;
she doesn't care who she hurts.

Out of habit, Clem quickly scribbled a list before she could sleep. No matter how tired she was, she needed to make a list before bed.

By the time Clem opened her eyes the next morning, the sun was already soaking the ground with welcomed warmth. She rolled over to a patch of white light that filtered through the fir branches, letting it spread over her like melting butter. Everything that had happened in the last day slowly came back to her. The incidents listed themselves in her head like a charging army.

I rescue Tong Ling.
Uncle Doran is lost to me.

Jed plows in both light and strong.
We are burdened with Sarah.

From the fire's ashes came a spicy-smelling stream of smoke lifting into the sky. Tong-Ling and Sarah were sleeping hidden under blankets, but Jed lay sprawled out on the ground, one arm straight over his head and the other tangled crazily in his shaggy hair. Jed's mouth hung open and his breath was loud. Clem had to laugh—she felt a real fondness for the sight of him comfortable and relaxed. She remembered Sarah and Jed together, Jed helping Sarah from the boat and making the bed for her. She wondered if she would lose this friend to Sarah just as she had lost her uncle. Suddenly Clem knew that even though she could not change her uncle, she could fight to keep Jed. *I will be as attentive and talkative as Sarah, only in my own way*, she promised herself.

Before she could finish her thoughts, Jed popped up, wide-eyed and awake. "Jiminy, I slept like I was in a deep hole. Why'd you let me snore right on through sunup?"

"I just woke up myself," Clem admitted.

At the sound of their voices a deer was startled in the bushes. It took off running, setting off an explosion of tree and wood sounds. Tong-Ling jumped out of sleep in fear.

"It's okay," Clem reassured him. "We scared up a deer is all."

Jed pointed to the sun above the high summit of the island. "Looks to be about nine already." Right away he started collecting what little they had brought ashore with them and putting it in his pack, except for the food. That he left out.

Watching Tong-Ling fold his blanket, Clem thought his

face looked better today, with less chalky white color around his mouth.

"Are you better?" Clem asked Tong-Ling.

"Much stronger," he answered. Clem could hear the ease in his voice. "But I cannot stop remembering the others who are not so fortunate as I."

"Who were they?" Jed asked, sitting down beside Clem.

Tong-Ling shrugged. "I did not know them well. I met them in the hiding caverns that are dug under the streets of Port Townsend."

"Right under the street?" Jed said, astonished. "I've walked directly over top."

"We were hidden there a week, and I taught them some English," Tong-Ling said, remembering. "They were new to this country and did not know it was illegal for them to come."

"No one told them?" Clem asked.

Tong-Ling shook his head. "The people who smuggle them in make much money. They will not say no. They will not stop."

"But you knew," Clem said.

"Yes," Tong-Ling said. "I knew." Clem could see sadness sweep over Tong-Ling's face like a sudden wind bruising the treetops.

Sarah finally stirred and Clem realized how late it was getting. Motioning to the others, she said, "We have to go."

Sarah ignored Clem's order and stretched leisurely. With the blanket half falling off her shoulder Sarah almost simpered to Jed. "This bed you made for me, Jed, did the trick. It's almost as comfortable as my old bed at home." She was quick to add, "My home with Father, before he died. Not the bed on Granger." She pulled her hair off her forehead, making it tumble in shiny waves down her back like moon paths on the water.

Clem unconsciously touched her own shoulder-length brown hair. No wonder Jed was ready to lay himself across a mud puddle for Sarah to walk on. Her voice dripped sourness. "Come on," she said.

Sarah quipped, "Why should I?" to Clem's scowl.

"Because you're here," Clem answered. She looked to Jed for help. He always had a way of touching a soft spot in Sarah that Clem couldn't find. But he turned away from them and began to scatter the brush they had slept on. Jed's busyness made it seem as if he was ignoring their exchange on purpose.

"The sooner we get to Whatcom, the sooner we won't ever have to see each other again," Clem continued. "Let's get this camp cleaned up." Her voice sounded like gravel in her ears. She saw Sarah's eyes narrow. She felt Sarah was spitting on her with just a look.

Sarah didn't waste time in replying. Glancing toward Tong-Ling but speaking to Clem, she said, "I don't know why you are so eager to help this criminal. He just sits there like he's dead already." She stood up, shaking the dirt angrily from her skirt.

Sarah's words crept through all the cracks in Clem. Was it wrong for Tong-Ling to come back to the United States? Was it wrong for her to help him? Clem knew her father would say it was always wrong to break the law. But Jed had jumped right into helping Tong-Ling from the very beginning, never doubting that it was the right thing to do. Clem envied his confidence. Jed didn't seem to use his brain to think about wrong or right; he felt it in his heart. *I think I can feel it in my heart too,* Clem told herself. *I want to help Tong-Ling.* Clem wasn't sure why, but the reason seemed to be taking form in her mind the way her lists did.

"You could help us load the boat, Sarah," Clem said as she folded the blankets.

"I don't care about this dead log," Sarah said, pointing at Tong-Ling.

"I am silent in the way a spirit is when it has no body," Tong-Ling told Sarah. "I left my home against my parents' wishes," he explained. He used his hand to brush the dirt out of his hair. "Many times my parents wrote to me asking when I would return to China. But always I wanted more money. No matter how much I saved it wasn't enough, and when I did go back it was too late."

Clem kicked at the ashes of the fire and scooped dirt over the few places that still smoked. Jed brought the bailing bucket up from the shore with water in it. He poured it over the ashes as she stirred.

"How?" Sarah asked as they all got into the *Fisherbird.*

"They were no more," he answered slowly. "My parents, the whole village was dead. A few wandering beggars had moved into the houses after the dead had surrendered them, but I knew no one."

"All dead?" Clem felt a fear squeeze her stomach.

"It has happened before. The sickness blows in like a storm. Our area was never wealthy. Poor earth with little to give makes the people an easy target for illness."

"Sounds like the cholera," Jed almost whispered. "My pa seen it back when he was a boy in North Carolina. Whole families dead in a day's time."

"There was no longer a reason for me to stay there," Tong-Ling continued. "I was alone. There still were no jobs, no land for me to farm. In America there is money. I can eat, but only the food for my body. My spirit starves. It is as if I am floating between lives, one for my body and one for my heart. They are no longer joined."

When he said this Clem knew why she wanted to help Tong-Ling. She too was floating. As she listened to Tong-Ling's solemn voice, a list took form in Clem's imagination:

Things That Feed Me
Book learning to feed my brain
Foods from the sea and farm to feed my body
Knowing home and family will always be here to feed my heart
And all of this combined to feed my soul

Changing the subject, Sarah pointed to the pack that held the end of the food. "Can we eat something?"

"We'll eat when we get the *Fisherbird* under way," Clem answered, her thoughts returning to their present situation. "The faster we get going the sooner this will be over and you will be free to do what you want."

"I can't wait," Sarah said. "You are the most disagreeable girl."

Clem looked away from Sarah to strengthen herself against the harsh words. She pretended not to hear.

Tong-Ling said, looking between the girls, "Usually life

takes family from us. Swept away into nothing like a snow slide. It is not often that life gives us new family. You could be family to each other."

"Well, life is going to give me all the family I need," Sarah insisted. "And it won't be her!"

Clem still would not look at the girl. "Let's head out," was all she said. She thought, *Sarah is one of those people who, instead of taking a trail through life, just stomp through the forest killing everything in their way. Well, she won't get me.*

"Good," Sarah said, taking her place in the boat.

"Sometimes it's a bit risky living with brothers or sisters. Kind of like dancing around a beehive. I should know, having three brothers myself," Jed said to Clem. Then he looked over his shoulder as if he didn't want Sarah to hear.

"I could never think of Sarah as a sister," Clem returned.

"My tongue's slow, but hear me out," Jed continued. "Like I was saying. Shuffling around a pack of kids ain't always easy, but looking from the other side of the trail, we all fill gaps for each other. And I am mighty glad for it. Why, right now little brother Jacob is putting to the plow for the first time. That's one reason I can have some adventuring. And my little brother Jason is just a dandy hand at cooking. He makes a stew that Ma shakes her head over and says, 'It's got to be magic.'"

"Enough, Jed," Clem stormed. "Sarah doesn't like me any more than I like her. So there is no way we are ever going to come to an understanding. Let's get this sail up."

The wind was whole and steady as Clem and Jed worked together to raise the sail. It blew over Clem's face and she felt washed. She imagined the air picking up all the particles of sadness and fear, tossing them away like empty clamshells.

Once under way, Clem pulled out her fishing line. She hoped the dried-out worm on the hook would still attract a fish. "Let's keep the sail trimmed loose," she said, "so we can go slow enough to fish."

"Fish!" Sarah's face grimaced.

"When you're hungry enough, it will taste darn good." Clem tossed the hook and weight over the stern of the boat. She trailed the line out, letting it fall behind in the slow wake.

"If we're lucky," Jed said, taking the line from Clem so she could hold the rudder, "we'll be roasting a salmon over the fire tonight."

As soon as Jed took the line from Clem, Sarah became much more enthusiastic about fishing. "Do you think you'll catch one soon?"

Clem looked on in disgust. She thought, *If the wind keeps up like this, we could make Whatcom tomorrow. Then farewell, Sarah. You can go to San Francisco or anywhere you want.*

After ten peaceful minutes Jed suddenly pointed south to Shaw Island. "Hey, Clem! There's a ship heading this way."

Swinging her head around, Clem saw the white sails of a schooner. She knew immediately. "It's the *Bull*." The words scraped against her throat, as if there were a rope being pulled out of her chest. "How could he have known? He couldn't have seen us last night."

Tong-Ling was silent, but he reacted by lowering himself farther down into the *Fisherbird*. Clem watched him try to become invisible.

"I knew it," Sarah said. She sat up straight, staring out

intensely to the *Bull*, as if her eyes could pull the boat to her. "Doran is coming for me. He's coming to take me to San Francisco."

"Whatever they're coming for, they're coming fast," Jed said.

Dropping into action, Clem tightened the sail to get as much speed as the wind would give them. The smaller *Fisherbird* groaned and strained as it heeled over and pushed against the sea. As Clem looked behind them, with the *Bull* in full sail, it felt like her little boat had to push through thick spring mud.

"It's as if he was waiting for us," Clem said.

"No, for me," Sarah insisted.

Clem was doubtful about Sarah's confidence, but what did she know about relationships like that? She wondered if it was really love for Sarah and not the search for Tong-Ling that brought the *Bull* skimming full speed.

"We'll never outrun them," Jed said. His voice took on urgency.

"No," Clem agreed. "The *Bull* is fifty-two feet long and can move faster than a hawk on the hunt."

As the *Doran Bull* came close enough to see in detail, Sarah began waving her arms over her head. "Here, I'm here."

"They know," Clem said.

"They've come to kill me," Tong-Ling murmured.

"They look to be flying," Jed added.

"There's only one advantage we have over the *Bull*," Clem said. "The *Fisherbird* can go in shallow. At least that will give us some chance." But Clem hesitated. Maybe she was wrong. Maybe Uncle Doran didn't mean them any harm and he really did just want to pick up Sarah.

"We'd better find the spot splits-quick." Jed's voice began to rise.

"Don't go in," Sarah said. "He's coming for me. I know it."

It is a possibility, Clem thought. Clem headed the *Fisherbird* toward the beach, just in case. If Uncle Doran were coming for Sarah and not Tong-Ling, he would soon have to slow down and come alongside. They would know without taking Tong-Ling all the way to shore.

Ahead there was a spot where the high tide made a shallow canal through two rocks. Perfect for a boat like the *Fisherbird* with a centerboard that could be pulled up. They would need only a few inches of water beneath them. The *Bull* with its keel drew exactly nine feet, three inches and not a quarter of an inch less. But Clem was wondering if there was enough time to get to the safe spot. She watched to see what her uncle would do.

Clem could see Uncle Doran's large body perched on the port rail, his arms stiff as if he were pushing the *Bull* along. She remembered an item from her chess list: *Never look at Uncle Doran's face because you won't believe he's out to take everything.*

Suddenly Clem knew Uncle Doran wasn't coming for Sarah! His whole look was fighting mad, not that of a hopeful lover. *No, he's out to win a battle,* she thought. *This is like a chess game. Uncle Doran knows he can beat me, and he's pushing his pieces right down on mine, like he always does.*

"Never look at his face," she whispered under her breath as she took action. She had to use strategy to her advantage.

Uncle Doran would expect her to act as she always did when they played chess—give in to his charge and surrender. She realized she had to play as craftily as her uncle did. What strategy would he use? she asked herself. Then she knew. She would hold her position and pretend she didn't even see him coming until the very last second.

The *Bull* caught a gust and bore straight down on them. Jed held Sarah by the arm to keep her from standing up in the boat. "I'm here. I'm here," she chanted in a whisper.

The *Bull* surged on, closer and closer to them. Clem could see the water lift under the bow in a white curl, and she knew Uncle Doran meant to scare them into stopping if he could, and to ram them if he couldn't. She watched for just the right moment. "Be ready to turn hard," she said, keeping her voice tight and in control.

Then, just as the hull of the *Bull* loomed over them, Clem threw the rudder hard right, causing the smaller boat to tack left. The *Fisherbird* lunged, throwing Sarah and Jed to the low side. Jed scrambled to the high end, pulling Sarah with him. Tong-Ling clung to the gunnels to hold himself in.

The *Bull* swished past, just three feet in their wake.

"He's trying to hit us." Sarah's voice drained away to a hopeless whisper as the *Bull* turned for another pass. "He's going to kill me."

CHAPTER 12

Ways to Show Love

Be honest.
Show all of your faces.
Make apple pie.
Add cream to any food, even clams.
Tell your secrets.

Clem headed directly for shore, the wind pushing straight from behind. In just a few minutes, she knew, the water would be too shallow for the *Bull*.

Clem's *Fisherbird* slowed to a glide as the wind was lost behind the hill of the island. She motioned to Jed, and he pulled up the centerboard, securing it in the raised position with wooden pins.

"If he wants to kill us, why doesn't he just shoot us?" Sarah asked in panic. She now stared at the *Bull* as if it were a hunting animal.

"If he shoots us and the bodies wash up on shore,

everyone will know it is murder," Tong-Ling said. "But if he swamps the boat, it will look as if we simply drowned."

Tong-Ling knows too well, Clem thought.

Jed took up the oars as Clem lowered the sail. They slid into the spot Clem had picked out. A passage of water slid between two tall rocks. "I'll take us right in there." He pointed ahead.

"Good, then Uncle Doran won't be able to see what we're doing." As they entered the protected spot, Clem grabbed a handhold in the stone boulder, bringing the boat to a stop.

"But we can't see the old devil-dog either." Jed stood up, trying to peer out over the rock to deep water where the *Bull* stalked. "I'm feeling too much like a furred critter, caught in a trap."

Clem noticed Sarah was still and quiet, her head bent over trembling hands.

"We better make a plan," Tong-Ling said. His voice was strong. And it helped Clem feel better, knowing he was now able to help.

She said to the others, "There's no anchorage for the *Bull* along here. It looks like the only thing they could do is anchor farther out and row their dinghy in."

"Then we'll see them coming," Jed said.

"What will he do to us?" Sarah asked in a hoarse voice.

Clem, Jed, and Tong-Ling stared silently in response to Sarah's fear. They all shared the question.

"He will kill Tong-Ling," Clem said. "And maybe all of us."

Tong-Ling pointed to a ledge with a red-barked

madrone tree perched on it. "Jed and I can keep watch for them from up there. We'll have a good view but remain hidden."

"They might just wait until after dark," Jed said.

"I don't think so," Clem said, trying to measure the next move. "Uncle Doran knows we'll leave then too. He'll make a move soon."

"The minute we know what Doran is up to, we scoot out and search for a hunkering-in place farther up the island's coast," Jed put in. "Hopefully it won't be more than half an hour."

"Right, a better hiding place," Clem concluded.

Tong-Ling nodded in agreement. He and Jed crawled up onto the shore and, staying low, made their way into the trees. A few moments later Clem saw them position themselves as lookouts.

Clem was left in the boat with Sarah. Clem watched her for a moment, but Sarah would not look up. So Clem took the bowline and made it secure to a log on shore. She did the same with the stern. Then she put the sail away and straightened the oars in preparation for a possible quick escape.

When there was nothing left to do, Clem sat down again in the boat and pulled out her pencil and her last scrap of paper. Clem saw the slow tears falling from Sarah's face to her lap. She didn't know if she felt sorry for Sarah or not. Instead of wasting time thinking about Sarah, Clem began a list of everything she needed to remember for a fast escape:

Have sails and line ready.
Don't just look for wind,

Feel and hear it as well.
Instead of trying to think,
Let the wind fill your mind.
Use the shallows, but don't hit a rock.
Don't, don't look back.

"What are you writing?" Sarah's voice trembled with tension, and Clem could tell she was barely able to hold herself together.

"Things that will help us get away," Clem said dryly. Her voice sounded so mean that she added quietly, "I'm sorry."

"I don't want pity," Sarah half pleaded, half growled. "My whole life, people have felt sorry for me. First, when my mother died, I was the poor little motherless girl. Then my father died and I was the poor little orphan. Now I'm the jilted bride."

"I loved him too!" Clem cried. "He was more than an uncle to me! He was the only person who made me feel as if what I wanted to do was good and right. He's the only one who liked me as me. But then you came. I hated you because all Uncle Doran could see then was the beautiful Sarah."

"I've hated you since before I even knew you." Sarah looked hard into Clem's face. The intensity of her expression surprised Clem. "Longer than I can remember, since my father became partners with Doran, all I heard was how great you were. 'Clem can fish, Clem can swim, Clem can sail any boat, Clem saved the goats.' He told story after story about you every single time he was in Port Townsend. And all I could do was look pretty."

The words slowly started to sink in. Clem was shocked.

She couldn't imagine Sarah being jealous of her.

"When I grew up I discovered that I could make boys like me," Sarah continued. "So when I came out to Granger I tried to get Doran to notice me over you. I did it on purpose. But I guess I just made a fool of myself. He never really loved me. Not like he did you."

Clem was embarrassed and confused by what Sarah was telling her.

"I saw him, Sarah," Clem said. "He did care for you."

"Not enough," Sarah whispered. "Not enough to matter."

"No. He didn't love any of us as much as he loved the idea of getting rich," Clem said.

Sarah started picking at the skin around her fingernails. "You can say, 'Oh, too bad, Doran's not nice after all.' Then you go home. I have no home to go to. My past has been buried, dead. He was the only hope for me."

"My mother liked having you with us," Clem told her.

"She feels sorry for me. It is still your home, your family, and your dream. I want my own life." Sarah's face was pale and stricken.

"If you want something," Clem said, reciting one of her lists to Sarah, "make it your dream. If it is your dream, then make it your life."

"My dream and my life just drowned in the water right on the other side of this rock," Sarah said.

Clem realized Sarah had spoken the truth. She had lost so much more than Clem could imagine. But Sarah didn't want anything Clem could offer.

Sarah said, "I'm sure my father could not have known

about the smuggling. He was always so honest. But he and Doran had an argument just before he died. Doran wanted money for something,"

"I'm sure your father didn't know they were smuggling," Clem said. "And Chinese workers were probably just the latest cargo." Clem remembered what Ray Chung had said. *They couldn't make money selling seeds and needles. What else did they smuggle? Whiskey? Opium?*

She and Sarah then looked at each other in gathering agreement for the first time. Ten minutes had passed when Jed and Tong-Ling peered back over the rocks. "The *Bull's* dropping anchor," Jed said.

Clem climbed up to the top of the boulders where she could see Uncle Doran and Ray Chung lowering their dinghy. "We'll wait," Clem said, "until the dinghy is just far enough away from the *Bull* to make it hard to go back. Then we make a run for it."

"To where?" Jed asked.

"From where Jed and I were watching, we saw a tiny cove," Tong-Ling said thoughtfully. "Just around the next point."

"But that's less than half a mile from here," Jed objected. "We're never going to get away from Doran by staying put."

"If Heaven's luck goes with us—" Tong-Ling started to say.

"And if Uncle Doran believes we're trying to outrun him," Clem said, finishing Tong-Ling's sentence, "we can duck into the cove without being seen. He'll think we're still up ahead someplace."

"By jiggers." Jed clapped his hands. "While they're scurrying back to the *Bull* in the dinghy, we disappear."

"What's going on?" Sarah joined them on the rock.

"Uncle Doran's coming," Clem told her. She said it almost like a question, trying to gauge what Sarah's reaction would be. Clem noticed Jed looking at her in surprise.

"You sound different talking to Sarah. Your voice—it's nicer." He smiled approval at her.

Clem thought, *Jed doesn't miss anything.* She said out loud, "We're going to try to make it to a hiding place without being seen."

To everyone's surprise but Clem's, Sarah nodded without argument.

"Let's wait until the dog thinks he has the scent," Jed said. "Hopefully we'll have him running in circles, chasing his own tail."

Clem took out her list and read over it again. She noticed Tong-Ling watching her. "I make lists," she explained.

"About everything," Sarah added.

"I think I found one on the little island where you saved my life." Tong-Ling took a piece of paper from his trousers and handed it to Clem.

The blue heron is like the storm sky at dawn.
The robin is the last wink of a sunset.
The red-tailed hawk is the first fan of a glowing sunrise.

"I must have dropped it," Clem said, embarrassed.

"It is very beautiful," Tong-Ling told Clem.

"It's just a way I use to remember different things,"

Clem said.

"It is more, I think. It is poetry," said Tong-Ling.

"I just make lists," Clem explained. But she was pleased with the compliment.

"Clem is as bright as a new nickel," Jed pronounced. "But we got to be going."

Clem focused on what they needed to do next. "We give them fifty yards." She could picture in her head Uncle Doran rowing with strong, swift strokes, Ray Chung in the stern studying the shore, looking for them.

"Let's float!" Jed jumped into the *Fisherbird*, bringing the lines and pushing off all at once. Clem set out rowing. She focused all of her mind on her arms, strong, smooth, sure. Nothing else would do. She felt as if her *Fisherbird* were working with her, using its own muscles to help them flee.

They slipped out from behind the rock just as it hid Uncle Doran's view from the other side. "If we can't see him, he shouldn't be able to see us," Clem said.

"The passage will look empty." Clem could tell that Sarah understood what they were doing.

"It will take them ten minutes at least to row back to the *Bull* and pull up anchor," Clem explained. "Then he'll head for California. Before the Revenuers catch him."

"He'll be gone?" Sarah asked.

"Yes," Clem agreed with her. She felt a piece of Sarah's loneliness.

"Let's be safe around the next point by the time they get a sail up," Jed urged.

Clem poured herself completely into rowing in rhythm with the *Fisherbird*.

CHAPTER 13

Where the Night Comes From

Hard from the east,
Pushing daylight into the sea.
From under logs and beach rocks,
Seeping out like a small trickle of water.
Bubbling out of the mouths of fish,
From under leaves.
From fear.

Clem silently recited an old list in rhythm with her rowing. It kept her arms moving fast. Minutes later they pulled into a cove no bigger than a pond. In the pale sandy soil of the beach, madrone and fir trees grew on the steep sloping banks that kept settlers and loggers from inhabiting this part of Orcas Island.

Clem breathed her words. "It's a magical place." As she spoke, a kingfisher took off from its perch on a branch and swooped over the undisturbed surface of the dark water. The sound of her voice mingled with whooshing bird's wings and swirled like a breeze around the enclosed bay.

"This place is deep hidden," Jed said, looking around.

"I do not think you can even see the entrance from out in the channel," Tong-Ling added.

"Let's hope that's true and Uncle Doran sails the *Bull* right on past." Clem glanced behind her as if her uncle might suddenly appear. As she did, she noticed a ridge of clouds building in the west like a wave growing to break on the beach. She decided not to mention the clouds to the others. Maybe they would go away. Clem rowed the *Fisherbird* against the pebble beach.

"We can only wait and see," Tong-Ling said.

"In the meantime, I say we find some grub." Jed buried his head inside the pack. "There's nothing but crumbs lurking down here."

"What will we do?" Sarah asked.

"We can get oysters off the rocks," Clem told them all.

"A cooking fire would not be safe," Tong-Ling said.

"No," Clem agreed. "We'll eat them raw."

Sarah's face instantly scrunched up in disgust. "Raw? I've never heard of such a thing. It will make us sick!"

Clem shook her head at Sarah's reaction. *She belongs in someplace easy, like San Francisco,* she thought. *Sarah would never make a good farmer.*

Tong-Ling added, "There are people from islands near my home who regularly eat raw beach animals."

"I'm game." Jed put his arms across his middle. "My stomach's shriveling up like a prune inside."

On shore Clem bent over and grabbed her new knife

out of the fish box. Holding it hard in her hand made all the memories of the day Uncle Doran gave it to her return. She remembered the silk shawl he presented to Sarah and how jealous of her she had been.

Thanks, Uncle Doran, she thought. *You knew this was a useful gift.* Clem realized that if she could go back to that day, she would no longer want to trade her knife for the shawl. Fancy dresses never fed anyone, although they did make good fire starters.

On the beach she led the others to the waterline, where the lowering tide was exposing hundreds of white oysters growing like hard lichens on the rocks. She opened the wide, sturdy knife blade and started prying open one of the shells. Finally it broke apart, revealing the slimy gray oyster inside. With her fingers, Clem lifted out the mouthful. "Who's first?"

"Miss Sarah, you step right up," Jed said, gesturing to her.

"Oh no, please," Sarah said. "I can't."

Without waiting, Clem gave the first to Tong-Ling. "Almost everything the sea gives us is good," he said, slipping it into his mouth and swallowing without chewing.

"He knows just how to do it." Clem was ready with another oyster. "Slide and swallow."

Jed looked at Sarah, but she shook her head. "Pass the little slimer over, then." He held the soft mass up to his lips. Hesitating, he looked at Clem and then at Sarah. Clem got an oyster for herself, telling Jed, "Come on, we'll do it together. One, two, three, swallow." Both Jed and Clem ate their oysters.

"Well?" Sarah peered into their faces.

"It's food," Clem told her.

"Jed looks positively green in the face," Sarah said.

"It's not bad once you do it," Jed reassured her. "It's made a nice, comfy lump in my stomach."

Clem handed both Tong-Ling and Jed another oyster. Then Clem swallowed the next one. Sarah watched hungrily. "All right." She gave in. "I'll try one."

Sarah took an oyster from Clem. They all waited as Sarah tried to work up her nerve. She stuck out her tongue tentatively, touching the small morsel. "It feels like a slug!"

"You can do it," Jed encouraged her. "Down the hatch."

Sarah swallowed. "Ugh. It's awful." And then, slapping her hand over her mouth, she gagged.

"It will keep you going," Clem said.

"Give me codfish, please," Sarah begged, still clutching her face. All of a sudden Clem and Sarah burst into laughter, remembering when Clem had thrown the fish at her. It was the first time they had ever laughed together. Clem and Sarah looked at each other in surprise.

Tong-Ling and Jed watched the two girls without smiling. "What's so funny?" Jed demanded, and then added to Tong-Ling, "Let's you and me go make sure the *Bull* isn't about to charge."

Clem collected enough oysters to half fill them.

It was only a few minutes when Jed came rushing back. "The *Bull's* coming up on us."

Clem and Sarah followed Jed to where he and Tong-Ling crouched behind the rocks.

The *Bull* sailed right on past without seeing the cove.

Clem, Tong-Ling, and Jed celebrated by slapping hands. Only Sarah was quiet.

While heading back to the *Fisherbird*, Clem picked up a few pieces of madrone bark off the ground. "I used my last piece of paper," she explained to Jed, beside her.

"I been thinking about those lists of yours," he said. "I like them; they're sorta like recipes for living. I never knew anyone who did fancy writing before."

"It doesn't feel like fancy writing," Clem said. "But it is like a recipe, I guess."

In late afternoon, after the *Doran Bull* had been gone from their sight for several hours, the four set sail again, heading east, straight for Whatcom. Clem watched the clouds, now darker, close in from behind. She hoped they brought only the usual summer drizzle and not big winds.

When they reached the east end of Orcas Island, the channel that separated the islands from the mainland opened in front of them. From there they could see the whole northern coast of mainland Washington. Mountains stood in ordered formation, one after the other like a family of giants, from the pale white summit of Mt. Baker to Mt. Rainer and finally Mt. Adams, a hazy distant cousin far in the south.

"There'll be a moon tonight to light our way," Tong-Ling said.

Rising in the eastern sky, the translucent orb drifted peacefully above Whatcom. Clem noticed Tong-Ling staring longingly at the land that was their destination. They could even see a tiny line of white smoke from the sawmill. But Clem doubted the moon would be visible to light their way for long. The storm clouds loomed closer.

Then, pointing to the closest mountain, Tong-Ling murmured, "The golden mountain. All of what we have suffered is because of my folly, my greed in wanting to come to this land. And what have I gained? Not only is my life burned away to nothing but ash, I have singed your lives as well."

"You came here like the rest of us," Clem told him. "My parents and uncle came from Scotland hoping to own a farm of their own."

"My great-grandparents emigrated from Ireland and Poland," Sarah said.

"And my grands, on both ends of the stick, came from England," Jed added. "It sure doesn't take long for those of us that cross the finish line first to get huffed and puffed about others coming along behind."

As they left the shelter of the land, the water instantly grew choppy. Clem had to hold tighter to the rudder against the wind. She looked worriedly at the clouds, it would be disaster to be caught out in this open water if those clouds carried a windstorm.

"I see him," Sarah called out suddenly. "There's Doran."

"Where?" Clem leaned forward to see where Sarah pointed.

"Heading south, away from us," Sarah indicated.

"If he turns west soon, we'll know he's going for open ocean," Clem said.

"Stay back until we know for sure," Jed suggested.

Clem again took measure of the weather coming toward them. The wind was stronger. Jed saw her and said, "We've got a different kind of company coming, don't we?"

"I think so," Clem admitted. She knew the feel of a storm.

While under sail, they watched in silence for the next hour. All the time Clem worried about the weather. Finally they saw the *Bull*, a distant white spot in the smooth grayness, disappear southwestward.

"There he goes to California," Sarah said quietly.

"Then we are free to cross the channel to Whatcom," Tong-Ling said. "I don't think we should wait."

"I wouldn't want to get caught out in the channel in a big wind." Clem was unsure. She knew that once they started, they could not turn the little boat around in big winds without flipping over. But she watched Tong-Ling shiver and saw how pale he was. *He needs to get to land*, Clem thought. "Maybe we can still outrun it."

As soon as Clem had taken the boat away from land, she knew it was a terrible mistake. The wind-driven clouds hit them from behind as hard as if it were the *Bull* ramming them. The tops of the waves turned white and grasping, flinging themselves higher and higher toward the top of the dory. Clem trimmed the sail down to keep control of the boat. Tong-Ling, Jed, and Sarah all braced their weight against the high side of the boat, helping to maintain balance.

Sarah yelled above the wind, "We have to turn back!"

"It's too late." Clem shook her head. "If we turn sideways to the waves, they'll flip us over."

To Clem's surprise Sarah didn't argue. She seemed to accept what Clem said and braced her feet against the tipping side of the boat.

The storm grew. Clem saw the fear she felt in all the

faces of her companions. But she knew that she was the one with sailing experience. She must remain calm and steady.

The trough between each wave deepened. As the small boat dipped, the land disappeared from view, only to bob into sight again as they reached the next watery peak.

The wind made it hard to speak, but Clem felt she needed to say something that gave the others, and especially Sarah, some reassurance. "When we get to Whatcom," she shouted, "let's catch ourselves a really ugly codfish."

Sarah reached to Clem, grasping her arm hard, "I'd like that," she said in return.

With Sarah still holding on to her, Clem saw the wave coming. She knew even before it hit that it would come right over their bow. "Bail!" she yelled.

CHAPTER 14

Mapping out a Journey

1st: Know where you are.
2nd: Have an idea where you want to end up.
3rd: Pick a direction.
4th: Stay heading that way.
5th: Avoid rocks, trees, and large holes.
Last: Write down what you see along the way.

Jed took charge of bailing. He knelt in the sloshing boat bottom and tossed pails of water out over the side as fast as he could. As Clem watched Jed's steady determination, she took courage. She remembered one of her lists about making a map and knew that finding safe passage through this storm was the same.

Sarah and Tong-Ling stayed stiff-perched, backs against one side of the boat, feet against the other, as if they could push the raging waves away. No one tried to talk now, especially as darkness and the hard rain soaked into them.

It took everything Clem could find inside herself to face each wave, to find the trail over it to the other side. She kept just enough sail out to allow her to steer. If the *Fisherbird* slipped a tiny bit to the right or left, the sea would come rushing in and flip them over.

Jed was just a shadowy outline in front of her. But without ever slowing down he struggled to keep the water out. As long as she saw his arm bailing, she too would keep going. Feelings of affection and gratitude filled Clem as she watched her friend work.

Finally, after hours of fear, they seemed to cross through an invisible door into calm. Now the air was quiet except for tiny wisps of breeze that slipped through the cracks and tickled at the back of Clem's neck like a ghost's breath. She allowed herself to slump over the rudder, just making sure the dark lump of land stayed in front of them.

Clem awoke with a jolt. She had no idea how long she had slept, but a drizzly dawn was fading in. The fear of not knowing where she was hit her like a cold wave. In front of them the mainland loomed high, no more than a half mile away.

"Where are we?" Tong-Ling's voice roused Jed and Sarah.

"It's not quite light enough to tell." Clem shivered with wet cold.

"How far to Whatcom?" Jed wondered out loud.

Clem looked behind them to determine where they were by the islands. The east end of Orcas, where they had started across, was clearly visible. "I think we're close." Clem was relieved they hadn't drifted too far off course. "There's the mill, right there." She could see the smoke rising.

Tong-Ling seemed to revive at the news. But Clem noticed Sarah shivering hard. She let go of the rudder and put the two wet blankets around her shoulders. "I don't know if this will help."

Sarah smiled in thanks.

Clem decided to make shore on a muddy strip of beach north of town. There the *Fisherbird* would be safe from the heavy traffic of ships, both sailing and steamer, that came and went through Bellingham Bay. She found herself looking for the *Doran Bull*. It was difficult to see each individual ship in the murky half-light.

"Tong-Ling?" Clem asked him as they watched the land ahead. "Will you stay here and try for work in one of the local canneries?"

"I wouldn't feel safe," he replied. "It is best that I go to Alaska."

"My pa said that up north the rivers are so thick with fish you can walk right across them like a carpet," Jed said. "He wanted to go there. But my ma, she won't live in all that snow."

"I believe there is still room for me there. I will be invisible with the other undesirables." Tong-Ling's voice was faint, as if his words floated in sea mist. He turned and focused his gaze back over his shoulder toward his distant home across the Pacific. "If I had stayed in China as my father wished me to do, they might have lived and I would have a real home."

"More likely you'd be dead too," Jed said.

Clem was surprised at the hardness of Jed's voice. It didn't fit with anything she had ever heard him say.

But Jed continued, "My ma always told us kids that it's our job to go out and find what we're supposed to do. That life ain't going to come knocking on the door. Go to Alaska, and I bet you can find a home."

The wooden buildings of Whatcom on the muddy hillside came into view. Farther south was Sehome Coal Mine and its docks, along with the fancier brick buildings of the booming town of Fairhaven.

Brown smoke from chimneys rose in small rivulets out of low-built log cabins that were difficult to differentiate from the mud. Farther up the hill, a few newer clapboard houses with gardens and neatly painted picket fences drew their eyes away from the poor shacks on the waterfront. In the streets they could see the mill workers and townspeople moving around.

As they drew near the beach Clem felt uneasy about so many people looking at her. She scanned the rain-slopped streets and the muddy people. She tried to talk herself out of her fear for Tong-Ling. No one's going to question us here. *We're just four more filthy, wet people.*

As soon as the boat slurped into the mud, Tong-Ling said, "This is where I leave you."

Clem knew right away he was not ready to start north. "Wait. We can at least help you find some dry clothes and food."

"I can't put you in any more danger," Tong-Ling said, shaking his head. "I'm leaving."

Jed said to Tong-Ling, "Food! Happy thought! I say we scurry on up to the store where it's warm and we can get some feed."

"Does anyone have any money?" Sarah climbed out of the boat onto the muddy beach without even noticing her shoes or dress. Her feet sank into the muck right up to her hemline.

"No, but Uncle Doran has a trading account here. And Mr. Zebbler knows me," Clem said. "I think Uncle Doran owes Tong-Ling some supplies and us a meal."

Tong-Ling hesitated, thinking. "I should not be seen," he said, watching the people warily.

"You're right," Clem said, glad that he would let them find food and supplies for him. "There's been a lot of Chinese trouble here. I heard my father and Uncle Doran talk about it."

They all began to pick their way up the sticky-mud beach toward town.

"Then we'll be needing to find a place to hide you," Jed said to Tong-Ling.

"There under the docks, below the mill," Clem pointed. "It might even be dry."

"If I walk in the midst of all of you and look down, perhaps I won't be noticed," Tong-Ling, said.

Forming a tight group around Tong-Ling, they began to wind their way past cabins and low-built dark saloons that crouched by the waterfront. Along the bank, outhouses gave off a foul odor that was only partly washed away with high tide.

Remembering the clean beauty of the farm on Granger eased Clem's thoughts and distracted her for a few moments as they plodded through the mud.

"At least in Port Townsend we have sidewalks," Sarah said.

"They sure could use something alive and green growing around here," Jed added.

"Just a few years ago this was all forest so dense you could hardly move between the trunks," Clem said. "The early settlers said it was like living in a cave. They made houses out of hollowed-out tree trunks."

The moment they were near the buildings, Clem noticed the signs tacked to posts and walls.

GET OUT CHINAMEN!

"Let's hurry and get you into a safe hiding spot," Clem told Tong-Ling.

They could hear the loud buzzing of a huge saw blade from the mill.

One hundred yards . . . seventy-five, she counted in her head as they approached the dock.

Suddenly another sound, this one like a herd of animals moving through dry grass, rushed them. The wind whooshed with the sudden movement of arms followed by heavy bodies, and there were Uncle Doran and Ray Chung. Ray Chung grabbed Tong-Ling from behind, holding a knife to his throat, while Uncle Doran grabbed hard onto Sarah.

CHAPTER 15

During Danger

See everywhere.
Hear everything.
Be invisible.
Survive!

In an instant Clem saw the chessboard laid out in front of her. Uncle Doran and Ray Chung had captured the situation. Clem, Tong-Ling, Sarah, and Jed were the chessmen, and there stood Uncle Doran, the queen piece, ready to take them captive. Once again Clem had been outmaneuvered by her uncle.

Beside Jed, Clem looked straight into Sarah's bewildered face. Sweat was breaking out on Tong-Ling's forehead. She tried to clear her brain. Finally she had to ask Uncle Doran, "How did you know we were here?"

Uncle Doran, amused, shook his head at Clem. "You still can't think beyond the next move, can you? I knew you were headed for Whatcom as soon as you turned your boat east."

Compared to Sarah, her uncle looked huge. Clem had almost forgotten how big he really was.

"But what about the Revenuers? Aren't they after you?" she continued.

Uncle Doran shrugged. "They don't have much of a case if there's no evidence."

Clem knew right away that Tong-Ling was that evidence.

"We're here to make sure there is no one to say anything," Ray Chung added.

Clem looked around for anyone nearby she could call to for help. But of course Uncle Doran had planned his move well: They were tucked behind a building, completely out of sight.

At first Sarah seemed as shocked as Clem was. Uncle Doran's arm slipped around Sarah's shoulder and began to caress her. He exuded confidence. Clem watched in horror as Sarah turned to Uncle Doran, leaning in to him with a sweet smile. "I knew you would come for me." She rubbed her hand up and down his chest.

Clem's stomach felt as if it were exploding upward into her throat. How could Sarah do that? Especially after she knew the truth about Uncle Doran. But there she was hanging on him, her voice rolling out like candy that was too sticky-sweet.

Sarah hasn't changed one bit, Clem thought, watching her. *She is interested only in herself.*

"Oh, Doran, you can't imagine how awful these last two days have been." Pointing at Clem, Sarah continued, "She made me go with them. And look, look what's happened to my dress and shoes." She delicately lifted her skirt to show him her muddy feet.

Uncle Doran laughed. "You wait until I'm taking care of you. You'll never be dirty again."

"Enough!" Ray Chung interrupted. He pulled roughly on Tong-Ling. "We have what's ours. Now let's get back to the *Bull*." He shifted his hold so that Tong-Ling was forced to walk in front of him. As he turned, Ray Chung nodded to Uncle Doran.

Uncle Doran immediately dropped his embrace of Sarah and clamped a huge hand onto one of Clem's arms and one of Jed's.

"I would offer you my arm, dear Sarah," Uncle Doran said. "But I must make sure my niece and her friend don't cause any more trouble."

"They did nothing," Tong-Ling said desperately. "Let them go free."

Clem could see Ray Chung tighten his grip on Tong-Ling as he said, "There'll be no more of Doran's mistakes for me to clean up after."

Clem looked to her uncle in question. "Uncle Doran, what's going on?"

Uncle Doran wouldn't meet Clem's stare.

Ray Chung led the group along the high bank that followed the beach southward. He kept a hard grip on Tong-Ling.

"What Doran should be telling you," Ray Chung said to Clem, "is that I own the *Doran Bull*. I give the orders. Doran gambled it away years ago."

"That can't be true!" Clem exclaimed. But even as her words denied it, she knew from her uncle's look and Ray Chung's triumph that it was.

"Why keep it a secret?" Jed ventured a question.

"Why?" Ray Chung's anger swelled like a huge wave. "Who would do business with a Chinaman, a rat-chewing Chink?" He reached out with his hand that held the knife and grabbed one of the anti-Chinese notices off a tree as they passed. Then he threw it down and ground it into the mud with his foot.

That was why Uncle Doran was so desperate to make money that he would break the law: to pay gambling debts. She looked to see Sarah's reaction, but Sarah was staring up the hill toward the buildings of the town. So Clem spoke to Uncle Doran purposely to hurt her. "Sarah's father found out that Ray Chung won your portion of the boat. And you had to keep him from talking."

Clem could feel Jed shiver across the foot of air that separated them. Her throat closed up, making it hard to breathe, and her face felt hot even with the cold drizzle coating her skin. She was too frightened to think in anything but murky, rotten pieces. Clem, Tong-Ling, Jed, and Sarah stumbled on, pushed by Uncle Doran's and Ray Chung's strength.

Finally Clem squeaked out the question that kept biting the inside of her chest. "You'd kill me, Uncle Doran?"

"No, no!" Uncle Doran insisted. "We need time to get away, that's all. We'll let you go, Clemmy. You and your friend."

"Yes," Ray Chung said. "Tell her what she wants to hear."

"You killed Paul," Clem said simply. "You killed the other Chinese that were with Tong-Ling."

"Not Paul," Uncle Doran insisted, looking at Sarah. He acted as if he didn't even hear the other Chinese mentioned. "We argued, and it came to blows. But he fell. Fell on the deck cleat. Smashed the side of his head."

Ray Chung added. "Yes, he fell as a result of your fist-smash to the chin."

Clem wondered how Sarah could listen to them describe her father's death. But Sarah still seemed to be looking at the town, not hearing what was said.

At that moment Tong-Ling stumbled and fell to his knees. He dragged Ray Chung partway down with him. Uncle Doran loosened his hold on Jed, reaching to support Ray Chung. As he did, Jed took a swing at Uncle Doran's face. Immediately Uncle Doran put out his thick arm against Jed's forehead, holding him at bay. Then he gave one punch that sent Jed crumbling to the ground.

Clem screamed as she watched Jed fall. Before she thought, she lowered her head and used it as a battering ram into her uncle's stomach. He sat down hard, air rushing out of his body.

"Jed!" Clem called, kneeling next to him, touching his forehead. A dribble of blood ran out of his nose.

Ray Chung regained his balance and pulled Tong-Ling back up by his hair.

Jed groaned, and Clem held his hand, telling him, "I'm sorry, I'm sorry."

Then she threw the words at her uncle. "Why did you have to hurt him?"

Breathless and hoarse, Uncle Doran held his stomach. "You are as strong as an ox."

"Come on," Ray Chung demanded. "Before somebody sees us and gets suspicious."

Uncle Doran climbed to his feet.

Then Clem noticed who was no longer with them. "Where's Sarah?" she asked.

Uncle Doran looked around in surprise, but she was nowhere to be seen.

"You fool, Nesbitt!" Ray Chung charged. "You had to have that stupid play doll. Now she'll give us away."

"No." Uncle Doran brushed himself off. His voice was still calm and sure. "She just turned scared. Or maybe greed kicked in when she realized I didn't have the money she thought." He roughly grabbed Clem's arm again. "But I know her. She won't put herself out for anyone else. She'll hide till she thinks we've gone."

Where *was* Sarah? And which was the real Sarah? The girl who had laughed with Clem over codfish? Or the Sarah who had hung on Uncle Doran when he had something she wanted?

Jed groaned and tried to sit. Uncle Doran pulled him up. Jed swayed, threatening to fall again, but Uncle Doran supported him with an arm around his waist.

"This is your fault," Ray Chung threatened Uncle Doran. "I won't let your stupid weaknesses get me caught."

"I'll find her," Uncle Doran promised. "As soon as we get our cargoes stowed on the *Bull*." He nodded toward Clem, Tong-Ling, and Jed.

Maybe that will buy us more time, Clem thought. She

didn't have a plan, but any delay meant they still had a chance.

But those hopes faded when Ray Chung spit, "Forget her."

Jed's nose still dripped blood, but Clem was relieved when he said, "I feel like the day Juny, our old mule, stepped on my head."

"Where's the *Bull*?" Clem asked.

Ray Chung pointed beyond the long dock near the coal mine. Clem saw a tight group of steamers waiting to load coal, but she didn't see the *Bull*.

"Tucked right behind the coal boats," Uncle Doran said.

As soon as he told her, Clem could see it, like a salmon wiggled in amongst a pod of killer whales. The sleek boat was hardly noticeable among the heftier, square-built steamers. She remembered the uneasy feeling that had been with her as they landed. Now she knew why. It was as if she had smelled the *Bull* lurking nearby all the time.

As they came closer Clem began to panic. "Someone will see the *Fisherbird*," she told Uncle Doran.

"We'll pick it up on our way out," he responded.

"It will make a good raft for you and your friend," Ray Chung told her. "We'll set it adrift in open water, see where the current takes you."

Clem looked in panic to her uncle. "Uncle Doran? Would you?"

He looked away without answering, and Clem felt herself choke on the truth.

They walked down the long wooden dock that extended into the bay where the *Bull*'s dinghy was tied.

Clem watched Ray Chung glance warily at the hillside behind them. She wondered what he was looking for. Then, higher on the muddy street, Clem caught a glimpse of someone with yellow hair. It was Sarah.

"There's that little witch," Ray Chung roared to Clem's uncle. "Doran, you take your niece and her companions to the *Bull*. I'm going after her." He sprinted back up the wood planks of the dock.

When he was gone Clem tried to delay her uncle. "What about your part of Granger? Did you gamble that away too?"

Uncle Doran's look was enough. "I'll win them back. I just need time for my luck to turn around. If you stay quiet, your father will never know."

Uncle Doran pushed Tong-Ling, Jed, and Clem ahead of him on the dock. Clem tried to look back to see what Sarah was doing.

Clem tensed as she saw Ray Chung approach the girl.

Running hard, Ray Chung got closer to Sarah. But when it looked as if he would run her down, four men stepped out from behind a building and grouped themselves around her.

Clem watched Ray Chung stop in surprise. Two of the men approached him. Immediately Ray Chung turned and started running back to the beach.

The two men chased after Ray Chung. They tackled him, making a tangled pile in the mud. Sarah and the remaining men were heading for the dock.

"What the devil?" Uncle Doran exclaimed, and he turned his back on Clem, Jed, and Tong-Ling to see what was unfolding on the beach.

Tong-Ling inched his way to the far side of the dock that hung over the water.

Clem and Tong-Ling looked at each other for a moment, searching for something to say. Clem saw the corners of his eyes wrinkle from a small, hopeful smile.

"I know which way to go," Tong-Ling whispered. And without another word he flung himself over the side into the water. As he disappeared into the dark water below, Clem felt a small particle of herself hit the water and began to swim away with the man. *Me too,* Clem said silently to herself.

A new determination took hold of Clem, and she could feel it fill her muscles.

"Get out of my way!" Uncle Doran turned back to her with a look of danger and fear on his face. He was going to make a run for the *Bull.* She touched Jed's sleeve and their eyes met in understanding. They rushed Uncle Doran, each one tackling a leg.

He fell face first onto the planks. Dazed, he tried to move, but Clem and Jed held on tight as he kicked and swatted at them. Clem heard the pounding of running feet coming down the dock. She kept her grip tight. Lifting her face against her uncle's struggles, she watched their rescuers approach. The lead man wore the shiny silver sheriff's badge on his dark jacket.

CHAPTER 16

Ways to Begin Anew
Read your maps.
Look ahead.
Get back on the trail.
Stretch your finger out and point.
Follow where it leads.

Clem held tight to her uncle's leg until the sheriff and a deputy pulled him to his feet, cuffing his hands behind him. The men immediately shuffled Uncle Doran up the dock. Ray Chung was also handcuffed and being held by deputies. It happened so fast that by the time Clem and Jed could stand up and catch their breath, Uncle Doran was already at the top of the dock.

Watching, Clem felt a sudden longing as she saw her uncle being taken to jail. Her love for him came floating to the surface. And even knowing all the bad he had done and the lies he had told, she wanted to run after him and hug him until the old Uncle Doran came out again.

All the things I have loved about Uncle Doran, she started to list silently to his back:

His laugh
His words
Teaching me to sail

She almost wished he had escaped. But then she remembered his horrible crimes and the mental list came to a halt.

Quietly Jed took her hand. "Wow! You are some partner," he told her in a shaky whisper.

Clem took a deep breath, swallowing her tears. "I couldn't have done it alone." She squeezed his hand in return. Jed's nearness almost immediately started to fill the empty space that her uncle had left.

"I knew, Clem Nesbitt, from the first time I ever saw you that you and me would click together like a wheel to a wagon."

Clem felt her smile sink roots all through her insides. Jed liked her. Liked her best. "Me too," she told him. "I'm sorry I couldn't say it sooner."

Together they watched Uncle Doran grow smaller and Sarah become larger as she slowly walked down to the dock. Sarah kept her eyes on Clem and Jed. Clem noticed even as she passed Uncle Doran her head stayed facing forward, as if he didn't exist.

Then, when she was beyond Uncle Doran, Sarah started running directly for Clem. Clem didn't know what to think, or what Sarah was doing. As she approached, though,

Clem heard her crying. Sarah threw herself toward them and Clem caught her in her arms. Her sobs called out, as if every part of Sarah were breaking like ice.

"It's all right. Everything's going to be fine." Clem tried to soothe her but didn't really know what to say. She felt herself begin to cry, crying from relief, crying for Uncle Doran, and crying for Sarah. She held Sarah tighter and felt the girl return the pressure "You saved us. You saved Tong-Ling." Clem's voice was shaking.

"No, no." Sarah tried to talk through her uncontrollable heaving. "You and Jed were the brave ones. It was you who gave me the chance to run for the sheriff."

Jed joined their hug, wrapping his arms around both Clem and Sarah. "I think you are the two most ding-fine girls I ever saw."

And then they were laughing through their tears. "We all did it," Clem stated as she realized the truth of her thoughts. "Each one of us, even Tong-Ling in getting away."

"He escaped?" Sarah looked around, noticing for the first time he was gone. "Just like that?"

"Yup," Jed confirmed. "He did what he was supposed to do, same as you, Miss Sarah."

Sarah turned to Clem as if she were asking if she agreed with Jed. Clem nodded.

Clem scanned the bay thinking she might catch a glimpse of Tong-Ling somewhere, in the water or on the beach. But there was nothing.

It was then that Clem heard her name being called.

"Clementine, Clementine."

She looked up and saw her mother and father dressed in

their rubber raincoats, rushing toward them. Clem went to meet them, leaving Sarah and Jed standing on the dock.

Her mother gripped her in more than an embrace. "Clementine," she said. Clem felt her mother shake.

"Uncle Doran's been arrested," Clem told them. She felt the shock tremble through them both, like branches breaking off trees in a sudden storm.

"My brother," her father said. "It is hard to believe."

Clem's mother said, "We went to the sheriff's office looking for you. And there was Sarah! She was so panicked. We knew there was terrible trouble." And even though she released Clem from her arms, she continued to hold Clem's arm as if she might try to get away.

"Uncle Doran and Ray Chung have been smuggling," Clem said.

"The stupid fool," her father swore. "The Revenuers, they came to the house the very morning you left. Found a dead Chinese man washed up on Lopez, they did. He was tied in a burlap bag. It was just like the bag in your boat, Clemmy. We took off looking for you right away. But I didn't think it was Doran."

"We rowed to San Juan at first light," Clem's mother put in. "But . . . oh, Clem . . ." She couldn't say any more.

"From there we took the mail boat," her father added. "Whatcom was the closest, but we would have continued on to Seattle if I hadn't seen the *Fisherbird* pulled up on the beach."

Finally Clem's mother found her voice. "How? How could you be doing this to me? I thought I would die from worry." Clem could see her mother stop and take control of her emotions. But she was shaking from anger and fear.

Sarah came to them. She was drying her tears as she started to speak. "Mrs. Nesbitt, you should have seen Clem. She did it all. She sailed the boat, outsmarted Doran, and saved Tong-Ling, the Chinese man. Please don't be mad at her."

"I can see we'll be having a lot to catch up on," Clem's father said. He put his hands on Mrs. Nesbitt's shoulders as if he could contain her trembling. "We talk better when we have settled down a bit more."

"She, my only child left to me," Clem's mother said.

Clem knew her mother would never let her out of her sight after what she had done. She wondered if she would even be allowed to sail the *Fisherbird* again.

"Well," Clem's father said, "I'd better go be finding out what's happening to my brother." Clem could see sadness settle in her father's face. "Then, as soon as everyone is dry and rested, we will head back to the farm. And get that young man home." He indicated Jed.

"I imagine my ma and pa are beginning to think I'm turning into crab bait by now," Jed said.

"From now on, you'll be staying safe at home," Clem's mother told her.

Clem thought, *She will never let me go to school after what I've done.*

They started up the hill toward the sheriff's office. Clem stopped to wait. Sarah seemed to be holding back, hesitant to join them.

Clem's father was uncomfortable and stumbled around for something to say. "I guess we'll have to be making some other plans for you, Sarah. Now that Doran . . ." His words drifted away.

"Your grandmother," Clem's mother remembered. "We could book passage for you to San Francisco right from here."

Sarah looked hard at Clem as if she wanted her to say something, but Clem wasn't sure what Sarah wanted her to say. It was clear to Clem that Sarah was begging with her eyes. Finally Sarah stammered, "I—I've never even met my grandmother. She's old."

And then Clem knew. "Can't Sarah go on living with us?"

Both Clem's mother and father stopped and looked at her, surprised.

Before her mother could form the question Clem saw coming, she added, "I want her to." On Sarah's face she saw relief, and she thought of what Tong-Ling had said: *It isn't often that life gives us new family*.

"I've never known two people who did better together than these two gals," Jed chimed in. "They fill holes. A hole one leaves, the other can fill, and the other way round. One can catch the fish, the other can cook it."

"That's right," Sarah said.

Sometimes, Clem thought to herself.

"But is this what you are wanting, Sarah?" Clem's father asked. "It's at times a lonely life on the island."

"Yes," Sarah told them, looking straight at Clem. "It's what I want."

Suddenly Clem was glad that Sarah would stay. She liked the arguing as well as the friendship. And maybe, with Sarah there, her mother wouldn't feel she had to keep Clem so close.

Clem's father reached out his big arms and brought Sarah and Clem into their welcome. "All right," he said.

By afternoon Clem's father had returned from the sheriff's office and they were ready to set off for Granger Island. Clem, her father, and Jed would sail the *Fisherbird* home. Sarah and Clem's mother would wait for the mail boat.

A bright breeze blew from the west as Clem sat in the stern of the boat, looking out into the islands. She could feel her skin soak up the wind, and it gave her more peace than she had felt since before she had found Tong-Ling.

Together Clem's father and Jed pushed the boat off the muddy beach. Turning to look at Clem, her father said, "You'll be having the helm, daughter."

"Me?" She was surprised her father would allow her. But she didn't stop to question him. She took the rudder in her hands and felt the boat she knew so well waiting for her to speak.

Clem remembered all of the decisions that she had made in the last two days. All that time she had been in command. Using her most confident voice, she called out to her father and Jed, "Raise the mainsail." The wind filled the little sail as soon as it was secured, and the *Fisherbird* glided out between the anchored steamers toward a clear channel.

The wind and sea together held the *Fisherbird* in their grasp. The boat tilted and began to pick up speed. Clem felt the competing forces push against the wood under her. It was as if the boat were alive; she couldn't help being convinced of that. It was her friend.

As they cleared the channel and set course for the islands, Clem's father moved closer to her. "When the new term begins, you'll be going to school."

"What about Mama?" Clem asked.

"We'll make her understand that you are old enough," he answered. "And capable of doing anything you have a mind to do."

CHAPTER 17

Home

Home is water and wind.
It is round islands speckled with trees.
It is birds soaring.
It is animals.
It is family.

The next two months were a quiet time of settling back into life on Granger Island. When Jed saw them he said, "Clem and Sarah work together like spit on a rag." And they did, some of the time.

"No, no, no! You're still doing it wrong," Sarah scolded Clem as they sat working together in the late afternoon. "You have to crochet four chains before going back through the loop. You know you'll be learning the womanly arts at school as well as science."

"If you would stop yelling at me for one minute, maybe I'd be able to concentrate on doing it right," Clem answered her.

"She is right, Clementine. You'll have cooking and sewing classes as well as numbers and facts," Clem's mother affirmed.

And you'll have Sarah to help fill the void here at home, Clem thought gratefully. Sarah's desire to stay on the island eased the pain of saying good-bye.

Clem reminded her mother, "I'll be home every vacation and every summer. And when I'm through, I'll be home forever. I belong to this island."

Now Clem watched her mother leave her own work to gaze out the window to the bay. "Here comes your father. And he has someone with him."

Clem went to the window to see her father row the *Fisherbird* into Nesbitt Bay. He was towing a small, dilapidated dingy behind.

"Jed's come!" Clem sang. She rushed out the door, not even bothering to pull on her boots.

"Jed! Jed!" She ran down the beach.

"Look what I fished out of the channel for you, Clemmy," her father teased. "This boy was doing more bailing than rowing."

Jed looked embarrassed. "My boat takes in so much water I think it would be a better crab trap than a dinghy."

Clem's mother and Sarah joined them on the beach.

"Clem can fix it up for you," her mother said.

"I hope you're planning to stay awhile," Sarah said, welcoming Jed.

"He won't be able to get away till that boat of his is patched," said Clem's father as he pulled the *Fisherbird* up on the beach and secured it.

"Then Sarah and I will start some supper," Clem's mother said.

"Did you find out news of Uncle Doran?" Clem asked her father.

"I did," he answered. "There was a letter. He has been moved to Tacoma for trial next month. You know, Clemmy, that you, Sarah, and Jed will be called to be witnesses."

"I know," Clem answered. Her fear welled up again like a sudden swell of water.

Jed said to her quietly, "You and me can do it." Taking her hand, Jed held Clem back as everyone else walked toward the house. "Will you take a walk with me later? Just you and me?"

"I'd like that," Clem answered.

That boy has eyes in his heart, Clem thought. She remembered how he had said she and Sarah filled holes. And they did. They didn't always get along, but her parents loved having two girls, one to cook and sew with and one who could take care of the farm. And her father was teaching her more and more about farming so she could take agriculture classes at school. It was good.

At the end of supper Clem's father said, "Something else came in the post for you." He pulled a square package out of his bag, handing it to Clem. "Addressed to C. Nesbitt and Miss Sarah."

Sarah came and looked over Clem's arm. There was no return address.

"It's from Tong-Ling," Clem said.

"He never even knew my last name," Sarah whispered. "Open it."

Clem untied the string and pulled off the heavy brown paper. Inside was a homemade book. The front and back covers were made of thin, flat pieces of wood rubbed smooth. On the front was a Chinese symbol carved into the center. Between the covers were blank pages of paper. Nothing was written on any of them. There was no note or inscription.

"It must be from Tong-Ling," Sarah said.

"To let us know he's safe," Clem agreed.

"Can I have a peek-see?" Jed reached across the table for the book. When Clem put it in his hands he said, "This is enough paper for a lifetime of lists and scribblings, maps and instructions." He held the book out, showing the first empty page.

"I don't understand." Clem's mother began picking up dirty dishes. "It must be some strange Chinese custom."

Jed smiled at Clem. "We know about it. Here's the first page for tomorrow."

Chinese first started coming to the United States in large numbers in the 1840s to work in the gold fields of California. From the very beginning they were treated with distrust and dislike by white residents. As their numbers grew, so did the prejudice against the Chinese, until violence against them became common.

In 1882 the United States government passed the first of a string of laws that continued until 1910. These laws served to restrict the rights of Chinese immigrants and United States citizens of Chinese decent. On May 6, 1882, Congress passed the Chinese Expulsion Act, which barred the entrance of any new Chinese immigrants and made it illegal for vessels to transport these workers. In 1888 Congress passed the Scott Act, which further made it illegal for Chinese workers who had left the country ever to return. It is estimated that the Scott Act cut off between twenty thousand and thirty thousand Chinese who were out of the country for a variety of reasons.

It was not unusual for Chinese workers to make a return visit to China to visit family, find a spouse, or buy land for their family after earning money in the United States. Many of these banned Chinese had built family and community ties in the United States that they wished to return to. Those wishing to return turned to the black market and paid ship captains to smuggle them back into the country. There are still secret hiding places under the buildings of San Francisco and even small Port Townsend, Washington, where illegal immigrants were hidden.

The smuggling of human cargo continues even today, sometimes under terrible conditions that my fictional character, Tong-Ling, endured.

- A note to the pronunciation of the Pacific madrone tree. I grew up pronouncing it *madrona* tree, and I imagine it was pronounced that way since the early days.

I would like to extend my thanks to the Whatcom Museum of History and Art for their help and support, as well as the people of the San Juan Islands for allowing me to add two tiny imaginary dots to their collection.

"Chinese American History Timeline." *Interactive Chinese American History: A Project of Asian American Studies 121, University of California, Berkeley.* http://www.itp. berkeley.edu/~asam121/timeline.html/. Retrieved December 1999.

Chinese Exclusion Act. 1882. *Documents Relating to American Foreign Policy—Pre-1898.* Vincent Ferraro Home Page, Mount Holyoke College. http://www.mtholyoke.edu/ acad/intrel/chinex.htm/. Retrieved December 1999.

Daniels, Roger. *Asian America: Chinese and Japanese in the United States Since 1850.* Seattle: University of Washington Press, 1988.

Kung, S. W. *Chinese in American Life: Some Aspects of Their History, Status, Problems, and Contributions.* Seattle: University of Washington Press, 1962.

Lai, Him Mark, Genny Lim, and Judy Yung. *Island: Poetry and History of Chinese Immigrants on Angel Island 1910-1940.* Seattle: University of Washington Press, 1980.

McCunn, Ruthanne Lum. *Thousand Pieces of Gold: A Biographical Novel.* Boston: Beacon Press, 1988.

Scott Act. 1888. *Documents Relating to American Foreign Policy—Pre-1898.* Vincent Ferraro Home Page, Mount Holyoke College. http://www.mtholyoke.edu/acad/ intrel/feros-pg.htm

Sung, Betty Lee. *Mountain of Gold: The Story of the Chinese in America.* New York: Macmillan, 1967.

Takaki, Ronald, and Rebecca Stefoff. *Journey to Gold*

Mountain: The Chinese in 19th Century America. New York: Chelsea House, 1994.

Whatcom Museum of History and Art: Photo Archives. http://www.whatcommuseum.org/archives/index.html/. Retrieved December 1999.

With special thanks to the Lopez Island Museum, San Juan Island Museum, Whatcom Museum of History and Art, and the Luke Wing Museum in Seattle, Washington.

NORA MARTIN

Nora Martin is the author of four books for young readers, *The Stone Dancers* (1995), *The Eagle's Shadow* (1997; an ALA Best Trade Book for Social Studies; a Bank Street College Best Book), *A Perfect Snow* (2002; a Pacific Northwest Booksellers Association Award recipient; a Junior Library Guild selection) and *Flight of the Fisherbird* (2003). Nora's books focus on the connections between nature and the developing character in the story. She is interested in the effects landscape has on individuals in shaping their beliefs, values and outlook on life.

Nora was born in Seattle, Washington, and spent her child-hood years exploring the beaches and hills on western Washington. She loved the outdoors and being an observer of the world. "I once brought a dead kingfisher for show-and-tell in second grade. I thought it was the most beautiful creature in the world. My teacher did not perceive it the way I did, especially the smell..."

Nora received a Bachelor of Education from the University of Alaska, Juneau, while assisting her husband Andy in his research on bald eagles. It was living in Alaska that led to Nora's first novel, *The Eagle's Shadow*. Since the Alaska days Nora and Andy have lived in nine different states, as well as Europe and Africa. Every place they have travelled Nora has combined her love of nature, teaching, and writing. She has worked with teachers in Soweto, South Africa, tutoring teenage boys living in group foster homes, and has worked in several public schools.

Nora now lives in Montana with her husband and two sons, Winslow and Haynes. She teaches middle school language arts, Library, Gifted and Talented Education (GATE), and conducts writing workshops for both children and adults throughout the northwest. She is finishing graduate work in creative writing and reading instruction.